My name is
Eric

My name is
Eric

REI KIMURA

HANNACROIX CREEK BOOKS, INC.
Stamford, Connecticut

Cover design by Clement Michael
Front cover provided, with permission, by Horizon Books of Singapore
Interior Layout & Design by Scribe Freelance | www.scribefreelance.com

ISBN: 978-1-889262-25-3 (hardcover)

ISBN: 978-1-889262-84-0 (trade paperback)

Published by:
HANNACROIX CREEK BOOKS, INC.
1127 High Ridge Road, #110
Stamford, CT 06905-1203 USA
www.hannacroixcreekbooks.com
e-mail: hannacroix@aol.com
Follow us on twitter: http://www.twitter.com/hannacroixcreek

LIBRARY OF CONGRESS CATALOGING-IN-PUBLICATION DATA

Kimura, Rei.
  My name is Eric / Rei Kimura.
     p. cm.
  This novel was published in Korean in 2008, first time it is being published in English and in the United States. Japanese author published in Singapore.
  ISBN 978-1-889262-25-3
  1. Dogs--Fiction. 2. Experimental fiction. 3. Singaporean fiction. I. Title.
  PL855.I5228M9 2011
  895.7'35--dc22
                                   2009046570

CHAPTER | One

My name is Eric. A piece of gilt-edged, important-looking paper says I am a male Pomeranian of retired champion and show dog bloodline. Place and date of birth: a remote dog breeding farm, deep inside rural New South Wales, Australia on the 16th of December in 1997. I thought I would live and grow old in that idyllic farm with its acres of space and rolling hills. So how on earth did I end up in a concrete jungle and a city state called Singapore thousands of miles away? This is my story.

I arrived with two other squirming, squealing siblings, forcing our way out of our mother's tiny, panting body without mercy. In revenge for the pain we had caused our poor mother, Nature thrust us unceremoniously into a sudden burst of white searing light to which our half-closed eyes were unaccustomed, so that our frantic squeals rose higher, to protest this sudden eviction from the shadowy peace and calm of our mother's womb. And that was that. Suddenly, without warning of what to expect, we were deposited into a frightening new world outside that safe haven.

A blurry sea of faces circled around us and shrieks of "Oh look, they are gorgeous, especially this one!" pounded our ears.

Good gracious, did these human giants have to speak quite so loudly? protested my delicate newborn ears. Indignant at this sudden intrusion into my quiet world, I filled my tiny lungs with as much air as I could and shrieked back as good as I could and then a small sweaty hand reached out to gently stroke my ears. It smelled of chocolates and candy floss and, to my surprise, a great calm flooded my tiny, flushed body, from this simple gesture.

It was as if some kind of magnetic power flowed between us and I felt loved, strangely reassured and protected. I didn't know it then but this was my first contact of what would be a life-long love affair with humans and it made me feel safe and comfortable in an increasingly perplexing world. I decided I was going to like these ungainly, loud-mouthed giants after all!

I spent the first few exciting days of my life getting to know a world that was filled with all kinds of strange sounds, sights and smells of life itself, in a curious mix of humans and animals on the farm. After the first week, I decided I liked humans a whole lot better; animals had their own hands full having to protect and fend for themselves and didn't have a lot of time left to care about other animals. Humans, on the other hand, seemed to make caring for us animals part of their vocation in life!

Of course I learned later that the care extended was not for free and had strings attached, but when I was just a week old, I could be forgiven for not knowing any of these things and having such a simple view of people, motives and life itself! To me, the farm was my home and the people who owned and ran it were my family. Later, I made up for lost time really fast by being suspicious of everything and everyone!

I didn't know at the time why my "family" had so many dogs and they all looked so different. I am long haired and round like a powder puff and I had all kinds of people crowding round me screaming, "Oh, look, he's so cute" till I got sick of the word "cute."

But there were lots of other puppies who looked positively ugly with big bulging eyes and flat, round and knobby faces with just two holes for noses, and others who were almost hairless and thin with their tails lopped off but people seemed to want them. The family in the compartment next to ours had six of the hairless, thin puppies with no tails and yet I could hear people drooling over those ghastly specimens with comments like, "Look at those legs and that posture, already showing the beginnings of perfect breeding and markings!"

Then one day a man came and took all the six puppies away in a large cage and I never saw them again. Their mother cried and whimpered for a few nights looking for them and even when she was taken away from the pens for nursing mothers, she came back to look for them several times till another family took over the place. That made my mother nervous and she started to keep us closer to her and cuddle us at night more tightly as if she was afraid that we were going to be taken from her, too. She seemed to know something about the whole set-up at the farm that we mercifully had no clue to.

People always seemed to be coming and looking at us and all the other puppies and sometimes we heard disturbing conversations like "This crop of puppies is the best and suitable for export." It was only later that I learned that Bill, the big, ferocious-looking man who owned the whole place and all of us, was a dog breeder and we were mere "commodities" to him. Our births were carefully planned and matched and we were born just to be sold as domestic pets in distant places; the stronger and more fit we were, the further we had to be sent away!

Although my two sisters and I had no shortage of admirers, I had one very special secret admirer: she was Sue, Bill's eight-year-old daughter, who was not supposed to play with us but she did anyway. Every day, as soon as the bright yellow school bus dropped her off, she would dash over to our pen, red pigtails flying and spend at least an hour or so cuddling me and tickling my belly till I collapsed in a tiny heap of puppy giggles and flailing small legs. She loved all the other puppies as well but I was her favorite.

Once, when my Mom wasn't looking, Sue even put me in the pocket of her school tunic and smuggled me into her room and, just in case I missed the warmth of the puppy pen and my Mom's tight cuddles, she made a little nest out of her blankets for me to crawl inside. I think this was the origin of my lifelong penchant for crawling into soft fluffy blankets as a substitute for my Mom's safe furry paws! Anyway, that was the first time I had ever spent a night away from Tracy, my Mom, and next to her, I loved Sue the most. She always smelled of chocolate and sweet candy floss and reminded me of the small sweaty hand that had stroked me reassuringly in my first few hours in a bewildering world.

When her father discovered her secret trysts with me, he got really mad and banned her from the puppy pens till she agreed to follow the rules. Snippets of their disturbing conversation still haunt me today.

"What did I tell you about not getting too attached to any of the puppies?" Bill thundered. "It's better for everyone this way because you know that sooner or later, they all have to go! We're running a business here, Susan, and not a pet sanctuary!"

"Go?" I thought to myself. "Where are we going?" I was so innocent and clueless in those days that I didn't know anything! I thought life could continue, lazy and idyllic like this forever! It didn't even occur to me that I had to be born for something!

But Sue didn't care what her father said. She continued her daily visits and we became so close that sometimes I forgot she was a human and not a dog! I didn't get along with my two sisters; they were competitive and could be real bitches, like their namesakes! If I wanted something, they would immediately decide they wanted it, too, and a fierce battle of wills would ensue, even at that tender age. I think they are the reasons I developed a lifelong phobia for other dogs and to this day, I cannot behave civilly towards another dog. There's always this feeling that I have to compete and fight to win.

But Sue was different; she never fought with me or competed with me for anything. Instead, she petted me, gave in to me, spoiled me silly with treats and let me do whatever I wanted! Even if she started out by objecting to something I wanted to do, I could always manipulate her till I got my way.ut eI swear Sue is another reason why I am today an expert on manipulating humans to get what I want from them!

But maybe she spoiled me so much because she knew that I would be hers for just a few short weeks before we would have to part forever. As I recalled, the early part of my life was filled with so many painful partings that I never recovered from the trauma of the word "goodbye." It just sets me off every time I hear that detestable word.

But for the moment, a tiny Pomeranian puppy hovering on the brink of life was oblivious to everything but the swiftly passing wonderful summer days of bliss and contentment, rolling in the grass, chasing butterflies and basking in the wonder of new discoveries every day. Breezy nights were spent curled up, warm and safe in my mother's arms or should I say paws? And caught in the magic of this golden life, I wanted it to go on forever!

Those peaceful days were clouded only by visits from a man who came to check us and shove tablets called "vitamins" down our throats. I hated those tablets as much as I hated the rough, hairy hands touching me and a few times I pretended to swallow them but as soon as his back was turned I spitted them out with spiteful relish. My first lesson in human interaction, "pretend to do what those humans want and as soon as they turn the other way, reverse it and do what dogs want," makes life a lot easier because they are stronger so they always win anyway. There's a lot of truth in the saying "If you can't win by fair means, win by foul means then."

In retrospect, I think I had to pay a price for those idyllic days of doing nothing, not even having to please anyone and generally just not earning my keep, and each day, payback time was drawing nearer, unknown to me. One day a lady came to the puppy enclosures with a notebook and pen and said to Bill, "We need six Pomeranians, four Terriers, two Boxers and a couple of Jack Russells, sturdy export quality only." She wasn't a stranger to the farm because I'd seen her around, on and off, always with a notebook and pen.

Bill called her Betsy and I think they had a thing for each other because once or twice, I saw them holding hands when Sue and her mother weren't around. That creep, Bill, I wanted to tell on him but nobody understood me, of course. I didn't like Betsy's rugged, predatory looks and one day I went up to her and relieved myself against her boots just for kicks but I was so tiny she didn't even notice! But Sue saw what I did and later we had quite a few giggles over it!

After the giggles, she sobered down, scratched my ears and declared solemnly, "I hate her too, Pom!" That was her name for me, just plain simple *Pom*.

I wanted to ask Sue why she hated the lady so much but she didn't want to elaborate and distracted me with a new game which I fell for immediately, of course.

I know I am an orange Pomeranian, whatever that is, simply because everyone tells me that but although the events of the next few days didn't really connect to make sense in my simple puppy mind at that point of time, the lady's visit and her request for "sturdy, export quality puppies" had somehow made me feel uneasy and sent a chill down my little spine. Besides, Sue seemed affected by it, too, and now she came to play with me more often.

I asked my Mom, Tracy, about it but like Sue, she too clamped up and refused to talk about anything! Can you imagine how frustrating that was for a little puppy, curious to know what was happening in his world?

Two days after the lady's visit, a few of us were selected, put into cages and driven some distance to a place where a man in white poked some needles into us. Although it was not exactly painful, it felt right and necessary to scream and squeal with pain, just to protest and make a point. I was so tiny I fit into the palm of the man's big, red, hairy hand and when he stroked my face with a stout finger that didn't smell very nice, some strong antiseptic, I think, my nose twitched furiously and I screamed even louder.

After the "session," we were taken back to the farm and returned to our respective mothers. The trip had tired my sisters and me out and we snuggled happily into our mother's welcoming paws, sucking hungrily on her nipples, feeling her life-sustaining milk flow into us, and luring us into a deep sleep. I trusted everyone and I never wanted my life or anything to change. I don't know what I would have done if I had somehow known that this was to be my last night with my mother and my two siblings together, as a family, and soon, I would be put through the most painful parting of all, the forced separation of child from mother.

For a dog, sadly, most partings are final; there is no such thing as "See you in a month or even a year's time!" and once I left her, I would never see Tracy, my birth mother or Sue, my beloved friend and playmate, again. I didn't have much of a choice; someone made the decision and I was just taken away from the people I loved without any consideration for my feelings.

Little wonder that for the rest of my life I would have this phobia of being parted from my loved ones even for a few hours because I am mortally afraid that I will never see them again.

The next day they let our mother feed and groom us as she usually did in the mornings but they kept us indoors and didn't let us scamper around in the yard. I saw Sue coming round to see us but her school bus arrived just then and she scrambled off to jump onto it. That was the last time I would ever see her and I think no one told her that we were being taken away that day so she probably thought she would see me when she got back from school, as usual. Sometimes, in a somber moment, I wonder what she did when she came back from school that day and found me gone.

A couple of hours later, we were again loaded into cages and although I wasn't happy about it because it disrupted my day, I wasn't overly concerned because I expected to be back by the end of the day as before. My mother protested at being separated from her puppies by howling her loudest but she was no match for her human masters and could do nothing. They simply took us away from her.

I was so tiny I could hardly stand up on my hind legs but I did, gripping the edge of the steel bars of the cage with my tiny front paws and heaving myself up to look at my mother standing at the door of our pen. The last I saw of her was that of any anxious mother, head erect, ears back, straining to look for us and nose twitching for our familiar smells. As the van moved off, I saw her running after us till someone scooped her up and carried her back to the pen.

"Don't fret, Mom. I'm just being taken somewhere for the day," I shouted out to her. "I'll be back before you know it, like before!"

I think she heard me because I fancied her eyes filled with

tears and her fierce barking died down to a mournful whimper.

There was nothing more I could do because I was in no position to control my own fate so I just had to wait till they had done everything they wanted to me and let me go back to the farm and my mother. So I lay down in the corner of the cage and let the gentle bumping of the van lure me into sleep. The whining of the other puppies soon stopped as one by one all of us succumbed to the therapeutic rocking of the vehicle that was carrying us away from our home.

A metallic squeaking of bolts being pushed back woke us up and like an orchestra, the whining and squealing started up again. Two men were moving our cages out of the van and I watched with horror as we were loaded onto a kind of conveyor belt moving us through some dark tunnel into an unknown destination. I was terrified of the dark even at that time and even though I didn't want to draw unwanted attention to myself, I simply could not control the howls of protest that rose from my little lungs, gathered speed at my throat and were emitted in an enormous explosion! I discovered that I had very vociferous voice chords that belied my size and in later life that would be both my curse and my asset. When I get excited, I just can't control myself. My voice chords seem to run away by themselves to great majestic heights and there's not a thing I can do about it, even if I wanted to!

I howled till we came out of the dark tunnel onto a huge room bustling with people. Someone came over to remove our cage and I was transferred to another smaller cage with my two other siblings. I was relieved because if I was going to have to make a trip somewhere, it was better to do that with puppies from home rather than strangers. That is the problem with us dogs, we never really know where we are being taken and we cannot fight what people do to us, we just have to trust our human handlers to be kind and humane to us and not to take advantage of our weak situation.

But in this case, I didn't have complaints; we were well taken care of, given plenty of fresh water and food and even allowed to stretch our tiny legs in a penned-off area of the room. I was fastidious about cleanliness even back then and having held my bladder the whole trip, was near bursting point. So I took the chance to relieve myself in a far corner of the pen so that I had the space to move as far away from my own mess as possible after that.

It was after we were re-loaded into our cage where a water drinking fountain had been installed and the floor was laid out with new clean sheets and a corner tray for us to relieve ourselves that the terrifying thought dawned on me that perhaps I had been wrong. Was it possible that we were being prepared for a long journey somewhere and not going back to our mother waiting at the farm? Was it?

A panic button had been pushed and, terrified now, I pushed my face against the glass panels of the cage to see what was going on around me. Someone was putting our cage along with a few other cages of yelping puppies onto a trolley car and moving us across a wide open concrete space to what appeared to me to be a huge metal bird. It was white in color with a red tail and had wings like the birds I had seen at the farm only this bird was so big it looked like the whole world to me! Of course I didn't know then that we were being loaded onto a plane which would take me away from my mother and the country I was born, never to return again. The rocking motion of the trolley car was beginning to make me sick and I missed my Mom and the comfort of home so much I began to cry.

I don't know whether they put anything in the milk they gave us before we left the pen but thankfully a pleasant kind of euphoria began to numb my senses and I barely remembered being literally fed into a huge mouth at the bottom of the big white bird. This and a hazy impression of lots of other animals, mostly dogs of various shapes and sizes, being in this room inside the belly of the white bird and a strange purring noise which seemed to grow louder by the minute was the last thing I recalled before succumbing to a strange kind of inertia and drifting mercifully into a deep sleep. After that, there was nothing but the silent and comfortable peace of oblivion.

I continued to sleep as the big white bird thundered down the runway and lifted off with a shuddering metallic retraction of wheels, leaving behind the land of my birth that I would never see again.

CHAPTER | Two

A *heavy thumping sound followed* by the impact of a hard landing woke me up and, unprepared for the sudden movements, I was thrown against the side of the cage as I tried to get up. The temperature in the room was comfortable but I was shivering because the noise that followed the thumping was very loud and it pierced through my ears like a violent shot of light. Terrified, all the dogs started to howl in unison and it was only when the noise had died down a little to a slow humming that I realized I was howling, too, the loudest voice in the whole orchestra!

I was so frightened that my bladder, which had filled while I was sleeping, threatened to spill over but with a supreme effort, I managed to control it. Even in such potentially life-threatening circumstances, I wasn't going to start peeing randomly all over like my sisters. It was disgusting. My retired show dog Mom's words on this subject floated all around me and were a comforting distraction from the harsh reality of my present situation: "Remember, my puppies, once you start a disgusting habit, you never shake it off and it stays with you forever!"

With the difficulty of a post-drugged body still in shock, I dragged myself to the tray at the far corner of the cage and relieved myself. It felt so good to release at least that tension but my heart was still thumping and I couldn't stop trembling. A big question was dancing in front of my eyes: where were we and what was going to happen to us? Suddenly, I wanted the safety of my mother and to feel the comforting beat of her heart against my ears so badly that I began to cry, the small bleating wails and whines that I learned later moved the human heart to my advantage much better and faster than all the threatening growls put together. I had always been carefree and happy at the farm so this was the first time I was crying, not the mindless fussing around but real gut-wrenching sobs.

The big white bird grinded to a halt with a kind of shrill screeching as if it were in pain and there was nothing we could do but wait to see how and when we could get out of this. There was a sudden silence as if the scores of animals held prisoner in that big room were holding their breath in one single joint effort. It was surreal and awesome how so many very young animals could keep that still, as if suspended in time.But we didn't have to wait long before the door groaned open slowly, breaking that magical moment and throwing all of us into noisy pandemonium again as we scrambled instinctively to get out. Several men leaped inside and started moving our cages as the open door blasted in a strong wave of hot air. But I didn't care about the sudden nauseating heat and humidity because I could see sunlight and a bit of sky at last.

At that moment that was all I wanted—to be able to see anything outside the four walls of the rooms and enclosed spaces we had lived in for days. I had been, till now, a child of nature and space and the confines of the cage was starting to send fierce claustrophobic waves through my body and working me up to a massive hysteria. I had this rising urge to scream and scream my lungs, my guts and everything out. I could see them all spilling out of my body and floating around me. Had I gone insane?

More movements and shifting around along endless stretches of conveyor belts and back to the four walls of another room where someone took me out of the cage and examined me all over, forcing open my mouth and shining a light into my eyes. It was disgusting and a violation of my dignity so I just had to express my displeasure by sinking my tiny but razor-sharp teeth into my tormentor's intrusive fingers. The yelp of pain and expletive that followed satisfied my wicked need to punish someone for everything I was going through and calmed me down for the moment. But the events of the next few days showed me that no matter what I did, in the end the humans always won because they were stronger, they controlled the world and its life forms and they could punish me back, tenfold.

Most of the dogs that had travelled together were separated at this point. I saw my two sisters being loaded into a separate vehicle and driven away, the last faces of family and familiarity taken away from me! I cried again as I watched the van carrying my sisters kicking up dust and disappearing into the distance.

Then it was my turn to be loaded into a shining new black Jeep together with five other puppies. I saw my much improved mode of conveyance as a sign that things were going to get better for me; I waited excitedly for the journey to end.

When it did, I discovered that my next stop didn't have any knight in shining armor to greet me. Instead, a big sign read "Grant's Pet Shop and Grooming Center" and the person who came out to receive our cages was a stick-thin youth with the most unhappy face I had ever seen who walked with an interesting sway of the hips and most certainly hated the job he was doing. My heart sank because my destination looked like exchanging one hell for another and I was right. I was still confined to a cage in the pet shop except that the cage became even smaller and the handling much rougher.

I spent the first day in denial of my new life at the pet shop, but by the second day, I began to accept the reality that the small cage I was sharing with two other nervous homesick puppies was my new home for the moment. By the third day, I also accepted the fact that I was being put on display for the people who came to look us over, make comments and then left, sometimes with another puppy.

I hated my two whiney cage mates but the young man who minded the shop had warned us about fighting so I decided to restrain myself and tow the line. The best bet I had was for someone to "buy" me out of the pet shop and being aggressive would not help at all. I had heard enough by now to know that everyone wanted only sweet-natured, placid and cute puppies so I had to keep my filthy temper under wraps, for the moment, anyway.

On the fourth day, a family almost took me but the woman in the group objected, "Pomeranians are too noisy! Let's get a beagle instead."

By the fifth day I was desperate to get out of that cage and my days were beginning to take on a meaningless routine of trying to look cute to make anyone take me away from the detestable pet shop where we were handled like commodities and put on display. And the cold, sad nights shivering in the dark, dreaming of another life running free on a farm where I had a mother and a friend called Sue. I knew I had to stop thinking about them because the odds were very high that I would never see them again but I couldn't, I just couldn't. One night I was so sad I curled up in a corner of the cage, tears streaming down my face and wished myself dead. If I had any means of killing myself that night, I think I would have done that!

Humans are not sensitive to the feelings of us dogs or maybe it's not their fault, they just don't know that we can hurt emotionally too. Look at Bill and all those dog traders. They just took us away from our mothers without a thought about how that caused us pain. No one stopped to think that we too can

15

miss our families and, at seven weeks old, we were just babies and needed the warmth and caress of a mother. As I crouched uncomfortably in that dark cage trying to ignore the faint aroma of urine in the air, and waited for morning to come to look cute and beg someone to rescue me from life in a cage, I thought wistfully of the contentment I had taken for granted, of sucking on my mother's nipples and feeling her warm wet tongue as she groomed me with fastidious care. I probably got my future obsession with cleanliness from her.

I woke to another listless day of watching and waiting and hoping that today would be THE day. I wanted to give up, to let go, become mad and be put down because I couldn't stand another day in that filthy small cage any more but I didn't because we are all survivors and hopeless believers in miracles. Yes, even we dogs believe in such clichés as the light at the end of the tunnel and all that inspirational stuff!

It must be the start of some holidays because a lot of people came to the shop that day and every time the doorbell rang indicating a customer, I stood up, pasted my tiny paws against the bars of the cage and tried to look winsome, screaming, "Look how cute I am! Take me home! I can dance, I can entertain you!"

But it didn't seem to work and the more I hollered for attention and danced to show off my entertaining skills, the more people shook their heads and said, "Pomeranians! Too yappy!"

By late afternoon, I was exhausted and resigned to another night in the cage when the door bell rang and a little girl dashed in and pasted her face against my cage.

I glared at her and snapped, "Go away! You don't want me, yes, yes, I know, Pomeranians are too noisy! Just go away and leave me alone!"

I felt the nasty impulse to sink my teeth into that perky little nose that was just inches away but I managed to control myself.

"Mommy," the little girl shrieked. "Here's a Pomeranian, just like Eric! Please, can I have him? "

Her mother came over and peered a little uncertainly into my cage and by now I had thrown my moods to the wind and inspired by hope, had taken up my dance and song routine again. When I get excited, I just can't help myself, the dance and song just comes naturally!

"Isn't it a little too fast, Tanya?" the mother said. "Eric just left us three days ago. Perhaps we should look at a few more shops and leave the decision to over the weekend?"

My heart sank. I knew that if they left the shop, they would never come back. There were, after all, many other pet shops they could browse through and the little girl would forget about me. Frantically, I pawed at the finger that was stroking me and looked at the girl called Tanya with appealing eyes that were filled with genuine tears at the prospect of another day in the cage. That did it. She was truly hooked and then she winked at me and proceeded to do her own version of the dance and song number.

"No, Mom, I don't want to wait till next week or go to any other shop. I want this one. He's exactly like Eric! Remember, you promised I could choose Eric No. 2 and I choose him!"

Embarrassed by her noisy tantrum that was attracting the attention of the other customers, Tanya's mother nodded hastily and my heart sang with joy. It was going to happen at last! I didn't know who the heck Eric was but he had saved my life, literally! Another day in the cage and I could have gone berserk.

It was only later that I found out that Eric had been their last Pomeranian, a sickly, pathetic old dog with the nature and temperament of an angel who had died just days before they got me. They missed him so much they had come looking for a replacement but they hadn't bargained on ending up so quickly with me!

Sometimes, when my human mother, Jennifer, gets exasperated with me, especially when I go a little overboard with the dance and song number, she will try to catch me in mid-dance and sigh, "Why can't you be a little bit more like old Eric? He was so sweet and such an angel!"

That really gets me and I stop dancing for a moment to blow out the gloriously Pomeranian broad chest I am so proud of and hiss, "I can't be sweet and angelic, woman! I am a man!"

But then Jennifer cuffs me playfully and squeezes the life out of me in her special bear hug, commenting laughingly on my retarded sense of humor and I know that she loves me to bits, dance and song and all. And heck, I throw all manly pride to the wind to go all soft and cuddly with her. In her own way, Jennifer really knows how to get me!

The bored-looking geek who attended to the shop and hardly cast us a second look most of the time except to yell at us to shut up when there weren't any customers around, came over, fully attentive, now that a potential sale was brewing.

"This one is a perfect male, just came in from Australia a few days ago. Perfect markings and posture, champion and show dog bloodline, too," he gushed as he removed me from the cage and placed me into the willing arms of the little girl whom we both knew was a very crucial player in this deal.

The girl reminded me of Sue and I stuck out my tongue and showered her with soft, wet puppy kisses. That did it; I had won her over and I knew triumphantly that when they walked out of the shop, I would be walking with them! My ordeal in that smelly cage was almost over!

Jennifer was a little more cautious and asked about my color. They wanted an orange Pomeranian, exactly like their old dog, she explained, and I was dark tan and nowhere near orange at all.

"Oh, that's okay," the geek explained. "Orange Pomeranians

are born black and tan and the color gradually changes to orange as they grow. Look at what his papers say, 'Red Pomeranian.'"

Thankfully, Jennifer accepted that explanation and anyway, the little girl called Tanya was holding on to me so tightly there was nothing she could do.

They moved to the counter to negotiate the price for me and pay up in exchange for my papers which proved my pure pedigree bloodline. Just in case, because there was still time for them to change their minds, I continued to butter-up Tanya, my savior, with lots of wet, loving kisses.

It was over at last. The money had been paid, the papers handed over together with two tins of puppy formula and the geek waved us off with the hypocritical parting words, "Bye, little fella! I will miss you!"

I squinted sullenly up at him in the bright late afternoon sun I had seen nothing of since I left the farm in Australia. Miss me indeed! In the five days I had been there, he had handled me like a piece of meat and never cast a glance at me beyond that! Once he had even screamed at me for making too much noise and threatened me with a piece of rolled-up newspaper, but well, on hindsight, maybe I deserved that but still, to make out a case of missing me was a little overdone!

But I soon forgot about him because all that mattered to me was that I was free of that cage at last and I was going to live with Jennifer and Tanya. I really didn't know who they were or what to expect but anything had to be better than that cage which barely gave me room to turn around!

Tanya was carrying me very carefully in her arms as if I was a piece of ceramic that would break at the slightest pressure and I licked her face vigorously trying to tell her, "Hey, lighten up! I'm not all that fragile and I don't break so easily!"

But she didn't understand me so after a while I gave up and

just let her do whatever she wanted. My first lesson of human interaction, that dogs and their human friends spend a lot of time misunderstanding each other so someone has to give in and go along with the other at some point and well, simply make the best of the results!

They took me home in a beautiful silver car with Jennifer at the wheel. It was the first time I had ridden in a vehicle without a cage but cradled in the arms of a girl who reminded me of Sue and my other life that I would never be able to share with my new family and I loved it! I fell in love with the smooth gliding motion of the car and the exciting scenery flashing by! The soft velveteen of the seats was like silk after the hard steel of the cages that had been my normal mode of transportation till now.

It was the beginning of my lifelong addiction to car rides and sometimes when I hear Jennifer shaking her head and questioning why I can't seem to get through a single day without a ride in the car, I long to explain to her about that first ride home with my new family and what it did for me. But she wouldn't be able to understand me. It's sad, really; no matter how much we dogs and our human family love each other, we will never be able to truly understand each other. It'll always be a lot of guesswork like when Jennifer or Tanya or the man of the house, John, says, "Oh, I think Eric is trying to tell us that he is hungry" or "I think Eric doesn't like this new snack" when I love it and am simply "saving the best for last."

You know what I mean? So close and so much love to give and yet I can't pour out my heart and soul to the most important people in my life!

But no matter how much we may misunderstand each other, the unconditional love and loyalty "till death do us part" that we offer to our masters gives true meaning to the saying, "Dog, Man's Best Friend."

CHAPTER | Three

My *new home was a* beautiful apartment set in lush landscaped gardens complete with a sparkling kidney-shaped swimming pool and artificial fountains and waterfalls. Although it was decorated in some charming, old world Victorian style complete with bow-legged wing chairs and heavy oak console tables and was comfortable and homely enough, I could tell by the haphazard way it was kept that Jennifer, my new Mom, was no domesticated woman.

That afternoon when Tanya picked me from the scores of puppies was my luckiest day because when you come to think of it, we can't choose our families. Someone just picks you up and says "This is your new family and this is your new Mom" and that's it! What if I had been picked by someone I hated and just couldn't get along with? I would have to suffer with that family for the rest of my life! When I think of that, I am just so grateful for the family who took me and showered me with love through all the crankiness and terrorizing they have had to put up with. I don't think I would have fared so well in any other family!

They took me on a tour of the apartment and made such a fuss over me that I felt like an emperor! Especially Jennifer, she literally dropped everything and ran each time I made so much as a squeak and incidentally, that very first day set the tone of our relationship. I knew straight away that I could manipulate her and turn her round my little paw in any direction I wanted! I called the shots and she ran; it was wicked and thoroughly shameless of me to capitalize on my new Mom's weakness for small furry things with big round eyes!

Whenever anyone complains about her way of handling and, essentially spoiling me rotten, I want to tell them to shut up because they don't understand that this is our special relationship and deep down inside we both know that she enjoys it as much as I do. It's just that for her own self respect, she has to make a big show of huffing and puffing about how I treat her!

This relationship with humans is as complex as the attempts made to simplify and downplay it. I can't seem to make them understand that a lot of times, they are wrong about me. I am not just a pretty, powder puff of a dog who goes round collecting adjectives like "cute," "beautiful," and even "noble." I have thoughts, opinions, feelings and yes, I'm intelligent enough to remember things, for example, I think about my Mom, Tracy, left far away in that farm in another world more frequently than anyone can imagine!

It's usually at night, when everyone else is asleep, when I have my own quiet moments and then I start to think of Tracy. I wonder about stuff like what she is doing right now. Did she still think of me or was she too busy with other new pups? Sometimes, a tear eases out of my eyes when I realize that it is over. I will never see her again or feel the warmth of her furry body pressed tightly against me and that unforgettable life-sustaining milk that flowed between our bodies bonding us as only a mother and child can be bonded. But I know I have to put Tracy, Sue and the farm in Australia behind me and move on. Jennifer is my Mom, now, and this is my home.

I was glad my early days were so filled with new experiences and activities that I had time to get emotional and sentimental only at night. That way, no one could see the dampness in my eyes because I hated to show anyone my weaknesses. Once, Jennifer heard me whimpering and laughing in my sleep because I was dreaming about the little field of wildflowers at the back of the farm and rolling in the soft grass with my Mom Tracy and two sisters and how we used to run in circles chasing our tails with the sun on our faces. The dream was so real that I could actually feel the grass tickling my body!

"Look, Tanya, Eric is dreaming!" Jennifer said, delighted, and added, "Sometimes I wonder, do dogs dream?"

"Yes, Mom, you bet they do!" I told her, a bit embarrassed to have been caught in a vulnerable moment. But she didn't get me, of course, and there will always be this quizzical look on her face every time I laugh, cry or twitch in my sleep! Pity! There are so many things I want to share with my family but we don't speak the same language so they can never understand even a fraction of the things I try to tell them. Now how frustrating can that be?

Jennifer said I hadn't been "house trained" and they were afraid I would pee all over the apartment so they put me in the kitchen that first night with a basket filled with soft blankets. But I hated being left alone and away from human contact and besides, I had no intention of changing a cage for a kitchen because it was still confinement so I decided to holler till someone came to get me.

"Let me out of here," I pleaded. "Just put a piece of newspaper in the place you want me to do it and I promise I won't pee anywhere else. I'm very tiny but I'm not stupid. I know I'm not supposed to lift up my leg anywhere I want! Sue already told me that!"

But they didn't know who Sue was and all the things I was trying to say or promise so I remained in the kitchen all night till they figured out how to "house train" me. Thankfully, they left the light on so I didn't have to make a fool of myself by howling in real fear of the dark.

After a couple of hours when I realized they were in another part of the apartment and couldn't hear me so I was just wasting my energy, I gave up and fell into a deep sleep. At least the kitchen was spacious and clean and a paradise compared to the cage home with its semi-darkness and faint urine and antiseptic scent of my past five nights! I shuddered. Anything was better than that!

The next morning there was a slight commotion because I was so tiny and had crawled so deep into the basket and got buried under the blankets that Jennifer and Tanya couldn't find me at first! With a wicked sense of humor I lay very still in the blankets and let them hunt for me for a good fifteen minutes. Good Lord, where did they think I had gone? Walked up the wall to reach the window above the sink, pry it open with my tiny paws the size of a teaspoon and flown out all five floors?

"The basket! Why didn't we think of it? He must be in there!" Tanya said at last and I flew out of my hiding place and flung myself at her before she could find me so that "officially" I had won the game!

I discovered something new about myself that morning: I am very competitive and I always have to win a game. If I lost, I growled, I intimidated the winner with my song and dance number, I snarled and sulked, I was what you would call a very bad loser! My favorite game was a kind of tug and win with one of my soft toys which I would offer to usually Tanya or Jennifer and we would pit our strength against each other, tugging and pulling till one of us gave way. I love that game because it gives me a chance to really flush out all the male animal aggressive instincts inside that I don't have any outlet for. If Tanya or Jennifer should win, I would bark and bully them into surrendering the toy to me and then I would walk away, declaring myself the winner. I really played dirty!

Jennifer and Tanya spent one whole day teaching me two things, my name and the place I had to pee and answer all other calls of nature. A piece of newspaper laid out in the service yard outside the kitchen was to be my "toilet." They spent hours rubbing my nose in my urine and taking me to the newspaper to show me where the "correct" place was.

Actually, I understood everything straight away but I let them enjoy their condescending game of teaching a raw, intellectually inferior puppy the ropes. I obligingly peed by mistake on the kitchen floor and let them rub my nose in it and bring me to the newspaper to show me where I had gone wrong. It was all a game to me and I enjoyed it thoroughly!

But after a few rounds I got bored with this game and decided enough was enough. I walked calmly to the newspaper lifted up my leg with perfect aim and they got the message that I was well and truly trained. I watched as they congratulated themselves without knowing that I had known right from the start what the newspaper was for and I had just been playing along to amuse myself and please them!

Next, they tried to teach me to recognize my name.

"Eric!" Tanya said, jabbing a finger into my chest. "You are Eric!"

"The thing to do," her mother added, "is to keep repeating the word till he recognizes it. Dogs learn this way, listening to the same word or command over and over again till they recognize it."

"That is not true!" I protested. Not only did I know the word Eric the minute I heard it, I even knew who Eric was, I had heard all about him in the pet shop that day they came to buy me so Jennifer's theory about dogs was not exactly right, at least not where I was concerned but there was no way I could make them understand! But humans seem to like it when we play the dumb game and "get the hang" of things after a while so they can congratulate themselves for having successfully imparted knowledge to a mere mutt! But really, dogs aren't all that dumb!

"Eric! Answer if you know your name!" Tanya coaxed.

I turned my face away simply because I didn't feel like answering and I was really annoyed they thought I was so stupid.

"You have to be patient," Jennifer said. "He needs time to learn. Look, he's so tiny that his brain is probably only the size of a peanut! Can you imagine the capacity of a brain that small?"

That remark really got me!

"Hey, woman, that comment about my brain wasn't nice! In fact, it's downright rude!" I screamed.

With an angry yelp, I dashed towards her and sank my tiny teeth into her hand but my displeasure, probably nothing more than an ant bite, didn't work on them at all! On the contrary, they thought it was delightfully cute and were excited that I had answered to my name at last. In their minds, they had won the day because they had successfully taught me to recognize my name! I was well and truly exasperated. When you are so tiny, even your anger is ineffectively interpreted as cute! In fact, everything about you is cute! I swore I would eat myself to a fine sturdy figure with the broadest chest any male Pomeranian worth his salt could have and then my displeasure could never be interpreted as cute again!

"Okay, time to stop playing games," I thought.

Just get on with it and acknowledge that wretched name and finish with this exercise before I invite more attacks on my brain!

I didn't even like that name because it reminded me eerily of another dead dog but I was stuck with it. I started out by being terrified that his spirit would enter into me and make an angel out of me, but that obviously never happened! Why couldn't they have called me something more romantic and macho like Trojan, for example? I groused.

Dogs don't get to choose their own names and I guess I had to be thankful they hadn't destroyed my masculinity with a name like Cookie or horror of horrors, Puffy, like the poodle in the apartment opposite was called! He went around with a perpetually vacant look on his aristocratic face and well, I guess you couldn't blame him, stuck with a name like Puffy and a collar shining with zircon diamantes! Compared to that, Eric was a sight better, dead dog or no!

Later, I decided I liked the name after all, especially when I discovered that Eric meant "king" in some Nordic language. Also, it gave me some opportunities to have fun, the kind of sardonic, twisted fun that I like to spew out whenever I get the chance!

Jennifer and Tanya take me to the Botanical Gardens very often and sometimes, just for a lark and to get some peace from the onslaught of the hated word "cute" from the joggers who stop to coo over me, I would disappear into a bush somewhere to hide. Eyes gleaming with wicked intentions, I waited while the two scouts rounded the vicinity, frantically calling, "Eric, Eric, where are you? Sweetie, please don't disappear like that!"

When the crowd of joggers and curious onlookers have grown big enough, I catapulted out of the bushes and landed at their feet, watching and laughing at the looks of first surprise, then amusement, on the faces of everyone who had expected Eric to be a hunk of a man and not this tiny, puffed-up dog no bigger than a large guinea pig! In my puppy days, I just loved to "shock and awe" anyone I could get my paws on, making people laugh was one of my favorite pastimes.

But I did often wonder how all of Jennifer's dogs came by this man's name, Eric. Well, it wasn't long before I found out

27

why! One day, a friend dropped by and, as usual, after she had passed my inspection and received my nod of approval which guaranteed that I would not keep her chained to the couch area, I stayed nearby, just in case she didn't follow our house rules. I heard her asking Jennifer why she called her dogs Eric and not some doggy name like Brownie or Snoopy or Jingles. Now that was something I had always wanted to know myself so my ears pricked up immediately from their idle position and I edged as close to them as the need to keep a dignified and aloof distance befitting a "guard dog" on duty would permit.

"Well, actually, I did it to vent my anger on an old boyfriend who had ditched me and naturally, I wished him all kinds of misfortune including going to the dogs" Jennifer explained. "His name was Eric, of course, so there. You have your explanation!"

"But that doesn't make sense," the friend persisted. "You're going goo goo and gaga over your dogs every opportunity you get and all we hear is 'Eric darling' and 'Eric precious.' That's hardly punishment for this man Eric, cooing over him!"

The two ladies collapsed into a heap of female giggles that can sometimes grate on a guy's nerves but this time, I sat up in my corner and barked my share of the merriment, "Well said, lady! Exactly what I was thinking!"

"I guess you're right," Jennifer admitted ruefully when the laughter and barking had died down. "But well, it's become a kind of family decision that all our dogs will be male, Pomeranian and named Eric. This little fella here is our Eric No. 2!"

In the end, I had to admit that the name Eric had a decidedly better ring to it for a male dog than the other neighborhood canines answering to Puffy, Scruffy or Spottie! And for a dog that couldn't choose his own name, I had to be thankful for small mercies indeed!

CHAPTER Four

At *the end of a week*, I was declared a faster learner than expected of someone with a brain the size of a peanut. But well, if they could see inside my "peanut" brain, they would find out that I conformed not because I felt I had to obey but simply because I wanted to, for my own convenience.

Take the toilet routine, for example. I do everything in the newspaper in the utility room right at the back because I am obsessed with cleanliness and want to keep the rest of the house clean for my own comfort. I can't even bear to leave the newspaper unchanged after I have done my rituals and will pester Jennifer, John or Tanya, until the paper is changed. But the rest of the family sees it as obeying a command and well, in this often misguided "dog man" relationship, the best policy most times is "if you can't beat them, join them!"

But they become a little uncertain of me when it comes to responding to my name. I am notoriously stubborn and a law unto myself. It is a, well, doggone duty of canines to come running to their masters when they are called but not me. I only go running when I want to and when it suits my purpose, otherwise they can call till they drop dead and I would still be stone deaf. This is the rule I live by and really, I don't see why I must drop everything and go running the minute someone calls me, I really don't!

They each had a different theory for my "selective responses" to this name calling stuff. John called me stupid but in a good-natured sort of way so I knew he didn't really mean it and even if he thought so, I didn't really mind. Tanya called it "trying to act cool" and Jennifer said I was purely stubborn and acting up.

After several more attempts to get me to be more enthusiastic about my name, the whole family just put it down to one of my many eccentricities which were beginning to surface as time went on, and didn't try to force me to answer when I was called anymore. Sometimes they just came and carried me over, it was a lot faster than waiting for me to do it myself! I can be a real pain in the neck when I want to and sometimes, I wonder how my family puts up with me!

Then there is the carpet and rug thing. I know I said I am a clean freak and will never ever consciously lift up my leg in any other part of the house except the newspaper at the back or a post or tree trunk outside but when I get near a carpet or a rug, something just gets me. I just go nuts and all my hygiene principles go literally to the dogs! The fibers of a carpet or rug just feel so soft and inviting, a lot like the grass in the fields back in Australia that I can't help it. My legs just seem to have a will of their own. Just give me five minutes flat and there will be at least one damp patch on the carpet. I feel awful and embarrassed about it later but I just can't seem to stop myself.

Jennifer loves having carpets and rugs round the house and I must agree they look beautiful on the creamy marble floors so she tried all means to discourage me from marking my territory there. There was this "undog" thing she bought from Japan that is supposed to give out an unpleasant odor that dogs hate. It didn't work because I was not in the least fazed by it. She tried to coax and cajole me, reason with me, brought John over to threaten me with his big man's voice, but that didn't work either so in the end, to save us a life of unpleasant damp patches and suspicious smells, she rolled up all the carpets and rugs in the house and sadly put them away.

I was glad too because I hated not being in control of my body and the way my legs just had a will of their own when they struck the soft pile of a carpet. It had frightened me! And it was exhausting, having all that conflict and cat and mouse game with Jennifer. But most of all, it was sad that I couldn't make her understand about the grass in the fields of Australia and why I braved her displeasure, John's thousands of curses and my own self-respect to litter those beautiful rugs and carpets that even I myself felt sorry for!

I spent the first week sizing up my new family, placing them in categories in terms of how I should form a relationship with and of course, how far I could get away with each one of them. By the end of that week, I already knew who was who in that family.

Tanya was my playmate who played with me whenever she had time or felt like it but when she had other better things to do, she didn't bother much about me beyond the airy "Hi, Eric!' and a careless cuddle or two. She was a bit like me and I was sure I couldn't manipulate her so I didn't even bother to try. We were, in a way, peers and understood each other perfectly, both young and self-absorbed with our own agendas. But she had saved me from that horrible cage at the pet shop so I forgave her for her nonchalance and careless treatment of me. But I couldn't depend on her for anything serious, that much I knew.

Then there was my Mom, Jennifer. She was the most interesting one because she just didn't know how to manage and control me. All I had to do was to whine or yelp helplessly and she went to pieces and in a test of wills, she always lost to me simply because she couldn't bear to push me, in case I broke. You could say she loved me to distraction and I shamelessly took advantage of that and brokered all kinds of one-sided deals with her throughout my life!

I'm lazy to a point and if there is any single chance that I can get out of doing things for myself, I will take that chance gladly. When Jennifer takes me for walks in the evenings, I bully her mercilessly. If I can choose between running on the rough, sun-baked road on a leash, panting away in the humid tropical air, at the same level as the car exhaust pipes hell bent on emitting and flooding my lungs with vicious carbon monoxide fumes, or enjoying the evening breeze high up in Jennifer's arms, I will of course choose the latter.

So I always make an issue of sitting down and refusing to budge and when she tries to make me walk by pulling hard on the leash, I squeeze her more by going into coughing spasms and predictably, she will immediately pick me up, shower kisses on me and I continue my "walk" cradled comfortably and smugly in her arms.

Even when I grew bigger and heavier and she had to shift me from one arm to another, I refused to relent and walk on my own, not even when a fellow dog walker tried to shame me into that by saying sarcastically, "I see your dog is taking you for a walk, Jennifer!" and the other dogs bark out similar comments.

You see, I can be very deaf and dumb if and when I choose to! Let the other dogs who can't get their owners to eat out of their hands huff and puff in the carbon monoxide exhaust pipe level air if they want to. I had "trained" Jennifer to carry me so I deserved to enjoy my "walks" in comfort!

But with Tanya and John I can never play up like that. They see through most of my ruses and even though I try the coughing spasms on them, they ignore me and continue to pull till I get the message that my games and deceptions don't work on them and I give up and trot quietly, if resentfully, after them.

When Jennifer sees this, she always complains, "I don't know how you do that! I can never get him to walk by himself and he's getting too heavy to carry! Maybe I should think about getting one of those dog carrier baskets."

She scoured dozens of pet shops, each time coming back with a doggy carrier bag or basket she thought she could put me inside and strap over her shoulder. None of them met with my approval and I rejected all of them. Today at least ten dog carrier bags sit in the store room waiting to be given away to some other more accommodating dog!

Dear old Jennifer! That's how you make it irresistible for me to bully you—instead of thinking how to force me to walk on my own, you think about how to make it easier for you to carry me! That's how you can never do it!

Jennifer mistook my smug grin for a sheepish sigh of apology and gave me a hug.

"It's okay, boy! Mummy doesn't mind doing it for her precious," she said, and I shuddered.

What a sucker! But how much I love her, my beautiful, beloved Mom and really, deep down inside, we both know that she doesn't mind doing it because it makes her feel, you know, so "mom-ish" especially as Tanya is growing up very fast and currently hell bent on fighting Jennifer's mothering instincts.

But I'm not like Tanya. I love being mothered and the best thing about us dogs? We never grow too old for as much mothering, hugging and cuddling as we can get and that's why I guess we make such faithful and loving companions—especially for women in need of a good object for their mothering instincts when the kids are all grown up and have fled the nest! I really can't understand how Tanya can find her mother's love so stifling. Why I can never get enough of it!

But I guess that's where we differ from human kids. When

we are taken on, we pledge never to leave our nests and our moms and dads unless we are thrown out, die or are put down because of terminal illness, and we keep our promises.

Well, they don't call us "Man's Best Friend" since time immemorial, for nothing!

CHAPTER | Five

When I was about six months old, my body began to undergo some radical changes. I lost my cute round puppy fat and began to grow overnight in haphazard ways, sprouting gawky, spindly legs and a sharp face that made me look like a fox and, horror of horrors, was I beginning to lose my broad stout chest to this new narrow, pathetic frame? I couldn't understand what was happening to me and didn't like it one bit. I harassed Jennifer endlessly for an explanation to these disturbing changes especially when my gums started to itch and I just had to sink my teeth into anything that got in my way—shoes, books, furniture legs, even metal pipes, Tanya's clips and combs. Nothing was spared!

Jennifer called it "stretching and growing longer and taller" but I wasn't convinced. Then my beautiful fluffy puppy fur began to shed and was replaced by some irregular outer coat springing up in all directions out of a more organized undercoat. Jennifer explained that metamorphosis away as "molting and changing fur" and I looked a sight!

People were beginning to compare me with the Mad Monk, Rasputin! While I used to strut confidently passed every mirror in the house, I now skunked by, hardly daring to steal a peek. Was I going to lose ALL the cuteness I had used to get away with murder? That certainly didn't fit my plans at all! Now that I didn't even have confidence in how I looked, was I going to lose my special skills of manipulations as well?

But wonder of wonders, the geek at the pet shop was right. Within a matter of weeks, my fur color started changing from its murky black and tan to a glorious orange. It was amazing. None of us quite knew when it happened. One day I woke up, stole a look at myself in the mirror, and I was orange!

Boy was I glad to get rid of that ugly dark color that made me look like, well, a mutt, for this rich warm, dazzling orange! Although I was actually beginning to enjoy wallowing in self pity, as the days passed, I had to admit I was filling out very nicely and taking on the shape of a truly magnificent young adult Pomeranian.

Even Tanya was roused from her preoccupation with her friends and diverging interests of the moment to make a fuss over me, especially my beautiful new color and markings!

Within a month, my "changing fur" process had stabilized and Jennifer took me to a groomer for the first time to style my coat. When we arrived at the groomers, my whole body grew stiff and I hollered my loudest because for a few terrifying moments. I thought they were taking me to another pet shop to what, sell me off to someone else because they had become tired of me? It looked suspiciously like the first pet shop I had been thrown into when I first arrived from Australia.

"How could they? How could they?" I screamed and tried to break loose.

Jennifer, bless her soul, realized my fears and whispered in my ears, "No, Eric, we're just taking you to groom your coat! Don't you want to look beautiful?"

Indignant, I glared at her, and shook my body in a huff.

"The word is *handsome*, madam, not beautiful," I growled.

I don't think she understood me but at least the ice was broken. I relaxed and felt momentarily ashamed of myself. How could I ever think they were going to sell me off? Where was this thing about trusting your family? I guess after all the shuttling to and fro, I had very little trust left but still, come on, dog, this is your Mom, Jennifer, here. What about a little faith in her devotion to you? Hasn't she shown you enough of that the last seven months? I mean, carrying you around when you have four perfectly good legs and hand feeding you when you know you are very capable of eating yourself! Hasn't she proved her loyalty to you?

The groomer, Danny and I hit it off almost immediately. He was gentle and playful but at the same time firm and he wouldn't take any nonsense from me. Any attempt to snap and I went to the stirrups which held my head up so I couldn't get anyone with my mouth. I hated that, it was so undignified, so I decided it was better to behave with Danny and let him do his job peacefully. I knew my place with Danny and he knew what put me in that place so it was a perfect relationship.

Throughout my life, Danny would be the only groomer who could take me and my nonsense. I want him to make me beautiful again when I grow really old and must make that last trip to the vet.

I am a very vain dog and like to look good but this time I didn't care what Danny did to me because nothing could be worse than my current "changeling" style. Although my color was absolutely dazzling, I looked like a dog which had been electrified with my outer coat standing up in all directions!

Still, I was hurt when Tanya and her insensitive friends giggled at me and made comments like, "He looks like Rasputin, the mad monk!"

"Hey, that hurts, okay?" I snapped back, narrowing missing one of the many female ankles circling me.

But they were right. Mother Nature had abused the fussy

good looks that set my breed apart from other dogs and I looked a real mess! I really needed a good grooming to set it right!

When I returned from Danny's, the first thing I did was rush to the mirror where I spent a good five minutes shamelessly admiring myself. He had done a good job and transformed me from the proverbial ugly duckling to a swan! Jennifer was watching me from a distance, highly amused, but she said nothing. The good woman really knew when to give a dog some space!

The mirror rewarded me with a face framed by a beautifully cut halo of fur and an outer coat that had been trimmed into an elegant rounded shape with a magnificent tail that curled proudly over a perfect back. I looked every bit the show dog Pomeranian of champion bloodline that was meant to strut around and not slink past mirrors and hide in corners at last! It had been a long month of esthetic hell!

A year later, Danny split from his partners and started his own grooming salon in quite a distant place and after a couple of times, Jennifer got tired of driving me there. So she decided, much to my annoyance, to try a new grooming center nearer the house. I didn't want anyone but Danny to touch my fur especially as instruments like scissors and shearers were involved so I gave so much hell to the new groomer that at the end of the session, she handed me over to Jennifer with the declaration that I was impossible to groom. She didn't have enough insurance coverage for multiple dog bites to continue grooming me.

Jennifer riled at me for a while for being devious, demonic and manipulative but in the end, I got what I wanted. She decided that the drive to Danny's new grooming center was far better than being threatened with a law suit for dog damage. After that, there was no more talk of trying another groomer nearer to home.

The volatile "changeling" days were over and from then on, I could only fill out, develop the firm, impressively broad chest, sturdy and yet elegant legs and the glorious mane and tail of a full-grown Pomeranian.

It was a great time to bask in the glory of the great number of admirers who stopped to peer and comment, "What a beautiful dog you have!" as Jennifer huffed and puffed with me, by now weighing in at seven kilograms and a dead weight, in her arms, on our evening "walks."

CHAPTER | *Six*

Before I go further, I think I should explain about my "song and dance" routine because it's so much a part of me that to leave it out wouldn't really explain who I am. You see, the enforced and very painful separation from my mother, Tracy, at the very tender age of six weeks had traumatized me so much I have what a psychologist might call " separation anxiety."

I hate being separated from anyone. I don't allow anyone to say the word "goodbye," be it friend, family or even foe without giving him or her hell. And I absolutely, positively hate anyone leaving me especially members of my immediate family, Jennifer, John and Tanya. I always have this phobia that every goodbye is a last goodbye and I might never see them again. You can't really blame me because the last time I lifted my tiny paw in a gesture of farewell to my Mom, fully trusting that I would be back at the end of the day, I never went back and I never saw my Mom, Tracy, again.

Instead, I was bundled into several types of conveyance including a big bird I now know was a plane and trundled thousands of miles from all that was near and dear to me to end up confined to a barely acceptable cage, in a stuffy cramped pet shop for days. Terrified of where I would end up but still knowing I had to end up somewhere, my only objective each day was to beg someone, anyone, to rescue me from that hell they called a "transit home" for imported puppies. I was only six weeks old, weighed less than 700 grams and hardly six inches long when I was put through all these ordeals, so I guess I am entitled to nurse a grudge against the finality of that word "goodbye."

Anyway, the fall-back of this grudge is that whenever I hear the word "bye" or someone, especially any member of my family, picks up a bag or even dresses to go out, something happens to me that I can't control. It is as if someone switches on a panic button and I fly into this towering inferno rage, so violent and so intense that sometimes it frightens me too, this lack of control and discipline. Did it mean that I was in some way psychotic, as Tanya once shouted out at me in frustration because I had embarrassed her in front of her friends?

This unreasonable rage just builds up inside me and my body goes involuntarily into this frenetic spin, round and round, while my voice chords seem to have been hijacked by a devil, hollering at top volume with spit flying in all directions and eyes popping to the maximum permitted of a Pomeranian. No visitor or family member has ever been able to leave the house without being subjected to my trademark "song and dance" number! And almost everyone but the stone deaf emerges from the elevators in a kind of daze that Jennifer laments as my song and dance "aftershock."

I know I shouldn't do that and it embarrasses Jennifer so much but I just can't help it. My family has learned to realize that and accept it. Now they merely try to minimize the trauma of going out by switching the English word "go" which I obviously understand from one language to another, but to no avail. From Japanese to Chinese to Spanish to Indonesian and most recently Korean, I learned them all in record time!

Once, after a particularly magnificent display, I quieted down for a moment when a coughing fit temporarily hampered my vocal chords, to hear poor Jennifer say apologetically to her

41

visitors, "I'm sorry about that. We've tried all means to cure him of this habit but nothing has worked as you can see! Every time we leave the house, we go through this gunfire and we end up at the parking garage feeling as if we've just emerged from a battlefield!"

I tried to justify myself to my family by explaining about the "separation anxiety" thing but of course none of them understood me till one day John hit on the theory that a possible explanation for my irrational behavior was the trauma of being taken from my mother at such a young age. Bingo, you got it at last! Sometimes humans can be so dense! I can't understand why it takes them such a long time to realize such basic facts!

When the language thing failed, they tried other means to "wean" me off this routine so that they could leave the house in a more dignified, less hurried and definitely more relaxed manner. Jennifer would give me one of my favorite, mega-expensive snacks imported from Japan but although it distracted me for a few seconds initially, I could not be cheated of my grand performance. She still left the house in full armor from the "battlefield" in the end! I think now they've given up and just turn ignore my "going away present."

They were more successful, though, in another trick they devised of walking me down together with their visitors so that I would be cheated out of giving them my standing ovation of a send off at the door. After awhile, I got wise to this trick but I let it pass, simply because I love being taken out of the house and downstairs for a walk and this excuse for some fresh air was as good as any!

Jennifer was delighted. She thought she had outfoxed me so to speak and I let her think that. Why burst the bubble by letting her know that she hadn't won but I had simply decided to let her win on this one because it suited me to do so! The poor woman had suffered enough, having to take all kinds of nonsense from me and I didn't want to push her too far. I am, after all, not the easiest dog to live with!

There is one visitor I particularly dislike, to put it mildly, and that is Aunt Meri, Jennifer's sister. The animosity started the very first time she came to the house when I did my "song and dance" number on her, the small one that I did for visitors coming into the house. She flung me away from her ankles and scolded, "What a nuisance of a dog, so badly behaved, you should have him put down!" As if that wasn't enough, she jabbed a finger at me and added, "If you don't stop that, I'll put you in the microwave oven and roast you!"

That did it. Such outright disrespect! I decided I would never forgive her and yes, I would do my best to keep her out of our house. She might have been Jennifer's one and only sister and only living relative but I wasn't going to have anyone come to my territory and threaten me like that. Was I livid!

I am very possessive by nature and I hate it when strangers come to the house and start touching my family's things or go to any part of the house other than the living room where visitors are supposed to stay seated and not touch anything! I am told over and over again that other dogs are not like that. They are supposed to be controlled and not to control the people in the house and their visitors but oh, forgive me, Jennifer and John, but I can't bear it when those strangers with their unfamiliar scents come in and touch anything that belongs to my family. I just can't let that go!

Once it got so bad that I was literally "confining" our visitors to the sofa in the sitting room, not allowing them to get up even to use the bathroom without being threatened with a few painful nips at the ankles.

John got so mad that he threw me into one of the bedrooms

and locked the door letting me howl and holler in angry protest in the hot, unconditioned room till I got exhausted and stopped. It was Jennifer who later stole into the room to switch on the air conditioner and secretly shove a few treats into my mouth. That's how Jennifer is; she just can't bear to see me suffer any kind of discomfort and humiliation even though we both know it's my fault and it's her way of telling me, "Let's just humor John and give him a bit of face in front of his friends, shall we? But we both know who the real boss is here!"

Sometimes I think Jennifer likes putting me up on that little pedestal and spoiling and pampering me to bits because recently Tanya can be downright mean and has no qualms about snapping at her mother to stop fussing round her. I hate it when Tanya does that and to cheer Jennifer up, I always let her cuddle me and coo sweet nothings into my face and only push her away when she goes really overboard.

If there is one person I submit to or at least put on a show of submitting to in that house, it's John. With him, I know when to stop pushing my luck before it runs out and I have to suffer the humiliation of being punished. John usually punishes me by hitting a folded newspaper very loudly on any surface he can find, a table top, a chair or even the floor and then sending me to a corner or under the bed to reflect on my misdeeds. I am never physically hurt by these punishments but the humiliation of having Jennifer and Tanya see me punished and sent to a corner is enough to make me think twice about pushing John too far.

Fortunately for me, John is usually quite lax about his role as disciplinarian of the family and I get away with blue murder most of the time. He has these spurts of energy and I only have to make sure I keep out of his way during this time and then I'm home safe!

But there is one thing not even John can make me do and

that is eat by myself the one meal of proper balanced dog food I have to take every night. I get by the rest of the day with generous helpings of the fantastic snacks from Japan that I am addicted to and can't get through a single day without at least four or five pieces. My best bet to get all the snacks I want is, of course, the long suffering Jennifer and just to get some peace, she usually gives in and digs into the packet she always has around her and tosses a piece at me, screaming that it's the final, absolutely final piece, as I run off to some corner to enjoy it and woe upon anyone who tries to take my snack away from me. But, of course, both of us know that nothing is ever final between Jennifer and me till I decide to declare it so!

I usually wait till she sits down at her computer table and then I park myself on the floor or on the bed in front of her and stare up at her with the deep soulful eyes I can produce like magic when it suits my purpose. I usually start counting and almost every time before I reach the number ten, she sighs resignedly and I will hear the familiar sound of the snack packet rustling.

I tried the same trick with John and Tanya but it didn't work. They had Eric-proofed themselves so well I couldn't crack their defenses! They would just let me sit there till I got tired of waiting and pretend not to see me slinking away after some time to lick my wounds of defeat. After a couple of times, I didn't waste any more effort and time on them. Well, I have this philosophy of "you win some, you lose some" so I can just shrug this kind of thing off and go search for an easier target, usually Jennifer!

I am notoriously picky about food and the first time I sank my teeth into the Japanese snack of dried extremely tasty chicken called "sasami" I fell in love with it and from then on, no other snacks would do. But these are imported expensive snacks in Singapore and at the rate I needed those snacks, John and

Jennifer would have to blow a large part of the family budget on that! So they tried other cheaper European and American substitutes but they tasted so awful, like pieces of rubber that I refused to even go near them. What did the manufacturers of those snacks think —that dogs have deformed taste buds—to produce these rubbery objects and call them "dog treats"?

My family couldn't understand why I found them so objectionable when all the other dogs didn't seem to mind. They tried all the different types, bacon, beef, chicken but I would have none of it. After all, when you have had champagne, you wouldn't want to go near cheap wine, would you?

Thankfully, Jennifer goes to Japan very often and she returns each time, her luggage bulging with packets of "sasami" dog snacks! When other people talk about their shopping sprees of clothes, shoes and electronic stuff in Tokyo, Jennifer talks about how much cheaper dog snacks are there! She must always make sure she has luggage space for at least fifty packets of "sasami" each trip and that doesn't leave much room for anything else! Poor Jennifer, the things I put her through.It's a wonder she still loves me to distraction because sometimes I don't even love myself!

I think my Mom has the patience of a saint. At about this time, Tanya was beginning to feel the first storms of teenage rebellion stirring in her and could throw really mean tantrums at Jennifer, which she would fight for a while and eventually give in to but Tanya could be really nasty to her mother. But then who am I to criticize her? I have my very mean moments too; sometimes I feel that is what moms are somehow empowered by Nature to do, take all that kind of crap from their growing children and dogs! But still, poor Jennifer!

Returning to the subject of my admittedly unreasonable eating habit, I just hate, positively, absolutely hate those canned dog foods made of unmentionable parts of other animals that everyone says is good and nutritious for us and no one, not even John, can just plop it down on a dog bowl and expect me to eat it! I need serious motivation to slurp that stuff down my throat!

Jennifer tried to wean me off hand feeding by leaving the food on a bright, attractively designed dog bowl and coaxing me to eat on my own but I refused to go near it. After an hour or so, she had to throw it away especially since in the tropics, food goes bad very fast without refrigeration After wasting several cans of expensive dog food this way, she gave up the battle and Jennifer went back to the habit of putting me on a chair and forcing the food into my mouth, spoonful by spoonful. I would struggle at first and then give in gracefully. Seeing that I had made even John succumb to hand feeding me, that was the least I could do!

CHAPTER | *Seven*

When I was about eleven months old, I started to feel some strange changes in my body and my emotions. They weren't unpleasant in any way but I didn't feel very comfortable with these changes. They made me feel vulnerable, weak, and in some ways needy and not my usual independent self.

I was coming of age and had blossomed into a fully grown fine Pomeranian male and I was experiencing my first sexual urges. There was always this full feeling in my groins that made me do disgusting things like rubbing myself against anything I could find, be it a chair or table leg or even Tanya's or Jennifer's legs! That gave some kind of dark pleasure and relief but I hated myself for doing that as much as I couldn't stop doing it! As I said earlier, I am a very clean dog and I hate mess and somehow these new disorientating feelings and sensations made me feel in some indiscernible way unclean, imperfect and well, messy.

Apparently the rest of the family thought so too because one morning I heard Jennifer on the phone speaking to my vet. She was explaining my condition to him and kept nodding her head ominously and finally she sighed and said, "Yes, I guess you're right, it's better to neuter him. I'll take him over tomorrow morning."

"Neuter" me? What was neuter? I knew it was something to do with controlling these crazy things I was doing but I didn't know what that involved and I pawed at Jennifer asking for answers but as usual she didn't get me! I just had to trust her and pray that it was something which would work for me and not against me.

Still, that night I worried about what "neuter" was and tried to tell Jennifer to postpone it and perhaps give me some time to think about it; the next morning was kind of quick!

"I'll be a good boy if you give me just a little bit of time to find out what neuter is," I promised, and that night I ate my dinner smoothly and without the usual fuss and games.

But she still didn't get it that I was afraid of being "neutered" whatever that was and merely patted me approvingly, "Someone is being an extra good boy tonight!" and that was that! End of discussion if ever there was one!

The next morning, she took me to the vet as scheduled and she could sense by my nervous barking and involuntary shaking that I was anxious about why I was going to the vet when all the vaccinations for the year had already been done and I wasn't showing any signs of illness. So she talked to me in the car at last about what "neuter" was.

"I know you're probably afraid of the operation as anyone would be, but believe me, it'll be better for you and for us too, and in the long run you'll feel much happier and relaxed, not frustrated and pent up like this! You want to be Mommy's little boy forever, don't you?"

I still didn't get it but there was nothing I could do but trust her. It's moments like this that I realize how vulnerable we dogs really are, how ineffective we are against the greater forces of our human masters and we truly do not have control or say in our fate or destinies. At home and most of the time, I manipulate Jennifer mercilessly but here I was totally at her mercy and dependant on her good will and better judgment of what was good for me! But I know I do and can trust my Mom never to let

49

any harm come to me so I stopped trembling and licked her face to show her I agreed with her decision to neuter me.

Dr. Reed, my vet, gave me his usual friendly greeting, "So how is our handsome Mr. Eric?" and that relaxed me. He kept talking to me as he brought me inside and stuck a needle into me even before I realized what he was going to do. He has a wonderful bedside manner, but I also like Dr. Reed a lot because he reminds me of my other life on the farm. Like Bill and Sue, he is an Australian. I feel wonderfully comfortable with him and it just shows how much my Australian roots are ingrained in me.

He was still talking as my clenched paws slowly loosened and I slipped away into a deep sleep. The last thing I saw was Jennifer's anxious face peering at me and her voice asking the vet, "He'll be all right, won't he?"

"Right as rain! You can pick him up at 5:00 p.m. this evening!"

After what seemed to me like just an hour of sleep but was actually three hours of being knocked out by general anesthesia, I came round, slowly and fuzzily. I felt awful and my mouth was so dry I could hardly open it. When I tried to bark, nothing came out because my tongue was in the way, stuck to the roof of my mouth. Dr. Reed's assistant appeared and gently massaged my paws. That felt good and got some blood circulation going but when I tried to get up, there was a slight pain in my groin area, not any great pain, just a dull ache and discomfort.

She gave me some water and I drank greedily, feeling the liquid loosening up my tongue and mouth. I tried to bark again and this time at least I managed to squeeze out some cross-sounding croaks but that was good enough for me! I might have lost quite a bit of what I suspected was my manhood but at least I still had my voice!

I was that weak thatI didn't even resist when they put me in

50

a cage to wait for Jennifer to pick me up. But as the effects of the anesthetic started to wear off, I began to feel more alert and restless. Where was Jennifer? Why was she taking so long, I growled crossly. I wanted the comfort of my own home and anyway, didn't she remember that I had a phobia about cages?

The big ugly clock on the wall showed 4:00 p.m. So it wasn't her fault. She'd been told to come for me at 5:00 p.m. but I didn't care, I just wanted to be angry with her.

By the time she showed up at the appointed time of 5:00 p.m., I was on tenterhooks with anxiety. Although I know I should trust my Mom, I can't help it. I just can't shake off this fear of being left behind and separated from my family. It's always on my mind, that it happened before, it can happen again!

Boy was I relieved to see Jennifer rushing in to get me and for once, I gladly suffered the embarrassment of being subjected to her pet names and baby talk in public! I'd forgotten just how she could really baby talk up a storm but instead of the usual "I don't know who she is talking to actually" response expected of any self-respecting male Pomeranian, I lapped it all up shamelessly, simply because I was just so glad to see her.

"Lord," I thought. "I hope this neuter business won't make me soft and turn me into a sissy!"

Although that night I turned in earlier than usual and didn't have much appetite even for my favorite snacks, Dr. Reed was right. By the following day, I had bounced back to life, twice my usual robust self, none the worse for wear except for a slight pain when I ran too fast.

In the days that followed, I realized that Jennifer had made the right decision for me after all. This "neuter" thing did a world of good for me. I didn't have these crazy, pent-up feelings and uncontrollable desire to do disgusting things with my body any more, desires that could not find any outlet and made me feel weak, vulnerable and begging for release. I felt like myself again, fully in control and proud to be, well, me again!

I know some animal activists disapprove of neutering, viewing it as some kind of abuse of animal rights. But really, believe me from the bottom of a dog's heart, if a dog accepts that he will spend the rest of his life being a domestic pet and man's "best friend" with no opportunities to find a normal outlet for such urges, except for commercial breeding purposes, it's much better and more comfortable for both dog and "his best friend" that he is neutered so no dark frustrations and physical urges get in the way. I know I'm a happier, less frustrated and much better pet after that!

CHAPTER *Eight*

Sometimes it amuses me to hear Jennifer and her friends discuss all kinds of myths and dumb beliefs about dogs and one of the most interesting is a recent debate and conclusion that we are color blind, that we can't see colors so everything to us is black, white and gray. I object to that assumption because I definitely can see most of the colors around me! I mean, if I had to live in a world without colors, life would be very gray indeed and there would be no sunshine and brightly colored flowers to pluck and destroy!

Of course no one believes or even understands me when I try to tell them so I will just have to wait for the chance to show them some day that our world is filled with as many colors as theirs is. It's hard to makes ourselves understood. I hear the Japanese are making a device that owners can use to interpret the barking and other noises made by their dogs, including facial expressions, but I don't know whether I will still be around when this wonderful creation finally finds its way to our part of the world. So hurry up, Tokyo, I can't wait forever!

Sometimes it frightens me to hear Jennifer talking about things like a year in a dog's life is equivalent to seven years of human life! That makes our aging process seven times faster and I'm terrified of growing old, breaking down and forcing my family to do the humane thing and put me down. I hear that's what happens to dogs when they are near death; they have to be put to sleep because of the pain, physical degeneration, and the suffering.

Then I ask myself, "Why the heck am I thinking of aging, death and all that kind of stuff when I'm still so young, a bull rearing to go at just two years!"

Anyway, the opportunity to make my case about the color blindness issue presented itself one day. My Mom, Jennifer, is a junior college teacher and she needs to get up very early to leave for school. So I have become accustomed to being her supplementary alarm clock, pawing or licking her awake every morning at 6:00 a.m. sharp. We have one very strict understanding, though, that when the calendar shows red, it's a Sunday and I never wake her because it's the only day in the week she can sleep in. I respect that and I've never been known to make a mistake about it.

The trouble started during the mid-term holidays when she didn't have to wake up at the crack of dawn to prepare for school. Every night, before I pop into her bed to sleep with her in air conditioned luxury, I always check the calendar that hangs along the passageway, the type of calendar where the days are torn off page by page each day. The weekdays are in black which meant I had to wake her up; red meant it was Sunday and I let her sleep on.

During the holidays, I continued to wake her up at 6:00 a.m. sharp because the calendar showed black. I got real frantic when she refused to get up and became very cross when I persisted. I didn't want to be accused of not doing my job and I was very hurt when she got so frustrated with my persistence that she flung a pillow at me and asked me to get lost. I went under the bed in a huff and refused to come out when she called me; let her be late, it wasn't my fault, and I had tried my best and got a pillow thrown at me for my pains.

If I didn't wake her up, I got blamed; if I woke her up, I got blamed, too. Who did she think she was? I was so mad that I contemplated going to the shoe rack and hiding one of her favorite shoes.

The next morning, because the calendar had shown black the previous night, I still woke her up at the appointed time and she tried to explain to me, it's something called the holidays and she didn't have to wake up so early. But I shook my head violently, really mad now. What did I do wrong? The calendar shows black so she ought to wake up and get to school!

Then Jennifer hit on a bright idea to get me to stop waking her up so early. She fixed a red page everyday to the calendar. The first two days I bought that and let her sleep in because I had checked the calendar the night before and it had shown red. On the third day, I figured that something was not right because Sunday had lasted a couple of days too long! So red calendar or not, I pawed her the next morning at 6:00 a.m. sharp with an angry intensity borne of the realization that I had been cuckolded!

I listened triumphantly later when my Mom Jennifer complained to Tanya, "I thought dogs are color blind! Then how did Eric manage to distinguish red from black?"

"So what does that mean, Mom?" Tanya replied. "That a dog can distinguish between colors!"

Well, I had proven two points to Jennifer: dogs are not color blind, and we are not all that dumb. We can uncover deceptions after some time! Although we settled this holiday "do not disturb" issue later by a good heart-to-heart chat, Jennifer could at least credit the dog who listened to her baby talk patiently most of the time with some brains in that tiny cranium!

And I went away trying to solve the enigma of Jennifer recognizing that I can see a red calendar and yet insisting that dogs are color blind!

It makes me mad sometimes to hear people say that we toy

breeds are not as intelligent as the big dogs because our brains are smaller! What about the TV programs we watch about the Pomeranians and Spitz in Japan who are used to alert their deaf masters and mistresses of telephone calls and visitors at the door? In fact, Pomeranians have very sharp ears—look at me, not a soul can get passed our floor without me knowing! It's just that I haven't been given the chance to work with my gifted sense of hearing because thankfully no one in my family needs that! But put to the task, I'm sure I could do it and sometimes I just wish I could find a job to be really useful! They're my favorite programs on TV, those documentaries featuring working dogs.

But sometimes I try too hard and too foolishly to prove myself better and stronger than the bigger dogs at the cost of endangering my own life. My Mom lives in perpetual fear of something happening to me someday on account of my foolhardiness and well, as self-fulfilling prophecies went, it did!

There's a German shepherd named Cole in the apartment two doors away and I absolutely detest him. He has this ugly, menacing look, slobbers all over himself, and positively stinks with a first class body odor. Don't get me wrong—he isn't a abused dog or anything; his owners adore him. It's just that he has a killer body odor that no amount of grooming, bathing, or perfuming can get rid off so they have learned to live with it and so have we, the neighbors, learned to ride in an elevator smelling of dog stink.

I can tell he hates me just as passionately and can't stand the sight or even sound of me. Maybe you can't blame him because of all the provocative insults I hurl at him from the safety of our closed front door whenever he passes outside on the way to the elevator. But I simply can't help it; if there is one dog I enjoy provoking, it's got to be Cole!

Outside, in the common areas, whenever we happen to even

catch a glimpse of each other, all hell breaks loose as we strain mutually on our respective leashes to get at each other's throats. He has that dark, smoldering glare that is a great advertisement for the saying "if looks could kill." My family lives in terror of the vision that someday the elevator door will open unexpectedly and Cole will dash out and tear me to pieces and you know what? One day, it really happened and I escaped death by a sheer miracle, although I did land up in the hospital with a badly fractured leg.

It was one of those damp, smoldering tropical nights and we had run out of cold drinks in the fridge so Jennifer decided to take me downstairs to get a cola from the vending machine at the poolside. As we were waiting for the elevator, it opened suddenly and, without warning, Cole lunged forward and, momentarily stunned, his owner loosened his grip on the leash. I felt myself being gripped tightly in the slobbering and powerful jaws of that monster. It had happened so fast that no one had the time to take any evasive action and I didn't know which was worse—the stench from that cavernous mouth filled with knife-sharp teeth that were sinking deeper and deeper into my neck or the pain of that deathlike grip.

Cole had been waiting for this moment to vanquish me for a long time and get even with me for all the insults and he was not about to let go. I struggled violently and tried to scream but nothing came out because he was forcing the air and the life out of me with his powerful jaws. I realized at that moment how small and ineffective I was against such a mighty force. All Cole had to do was sink his teeth deeper into me and cut through all my vital nerves and veins and I would bleed to death. It was clear he had every intention of doing that and I thought it was over for me!

I was no hero and I didn't want to die, especially not this

way! By now I was choking and losing consciousness from the struggle to breathe. And then, the miracle that a bad dog like me surely didn't deserve happened as Cole's owner came out of his shock and aimed a kick at Cole's groin. With a huge yelp of pain and surprise, Cole relaxed his grip and I struggled free and ran blindly away, anywhere, as long as it was away from that slobbering monster. I didn't notice the pain in my body and in my lungs as the air rushed in. Weakened by my ordeal, I missed a step and rolled down the stairs with Jennifer running after me, screaming hysterically.

I landed at the bottom of the stairs in a heap of blood-matted fur and thrashing limbs. Cole's teeth and vicious shaking had punctured my neck and blood was oozing out. A few minutes more and he would have fatally snapped my neck—I had been that close to death!

Jennifer bent down and gently lifted me up in her arms. She was crying because she thought I was dead or dying. But when I struggled into a more comfortable position and whimpered for all I was worth, she realized that I was very badly bruised possibly with a broken limb but I was going to be all right.

"You're a fighter, Eric," she whispered to me. "Come on, you can fight this one out!"

John had reached us followed closely followed by Andrea, the visibly shaken wife of Cole's owner, asking anxiously, "Is Eric okay? Please take him to the vet and send the bill to us. We are so sorry. I don't know what got into Cole! He usually isn't like that!"

"Like real he isn't," I whimpered feebly. "Have you seen those murderous looks? He was just waiting for this moment to nail me!"

I knew from the sparks of anger and my spirited protest against Andrea's unfair denial of her dog's savage streaks that although I was in real pain and suffering from the injuries Cole had inflicted on me, I was going to live and at that moment nothing else mattered!

I survived that savage attack with a broken front leg which had me hobbling in a cast for almost two weeks and a traumatized neck with internal bleeding under the skin that alternated between hurting and itching for almost a week. I was a broken dog and deeply depressed for the next two weeks and my family spoiled me horribly, catering to my every whim, but I was too down to even take advantage of that and exploit the situation to the fullest as I would have done in normal circumstances. I didn't even have enough energy to clean myself properly; and Jennifer had to do it for me, using a soft wet cloth to wipe away the deposits that tend to build up in a Pomeranian's eyes.

I was really down and out and the only time I would struggle out of my inertia was when I heard Cole walking past our door and I would spit profanities at him. How dare he walk the earth on four good legs while I hobbled around, helpless as a baby? Wasn't there a law against such dogs?

The cast was hard and uncomfortable, and so was trying to walk on three legs. But after a few days, I managed to limp around and by the end of the week I was running expertly on my three good legs with the front leg in the cast sticking out like a piece of wood. Tanya and her friends called me the dog with the wooden leg and wrote all kinds of things on my cast. I took it all in good stride and I realized that my brush with death had made me less sensitive and more able to laugh at myself or allow others to do so.

When the cast was finally taken out, I almost missed it because of all the attention I had been getting and the perks that came with invalid status. But all the good things of a bad event must come to an end. Today I have a leg held together at the joint by metal screws, thanks to Cole. Far from being intimidated and cowed by the incident, I hated Cole with even greater passion. Although I was more cautious now about challenging him except from behind the safety of my closed front door or from a safe distance fully protected by whichever member of my family I was with, I never missed an opportunity to irritate him with the shrill insults he hated so much.

"Ugly, smelly, slobbering buffalo," I shrieked whenever I picked up his scent.

"Useless toy dog, I'll get you the next time," he snarled back.

From a very safe distance from each, Jennifer and Cole's owners, Ben and his wife, Andrea, would shake their heads and say, "Those two, trading insults like two competing salesmen!"

A year later, Cole and his owners moved away, much to my family's relief. You might think I would be happy to be rid of Cole but strangely, I kind of missed having someone to spit at and trade insults with, and life became quieter on our floor.

CHAPTER | Nine

My family hoped and thought that I had learned a bitter lesson from this life-threatening incident but no, to their disappointment, I continued right on to challenge dogs three or four times bigger than me. Fortunately for me, these have been gentler and sweeter breeds like Labradors and Golden Retrievers who merely look at the little thug dancing round their feet quizzically and step back good naturedly! So I live to bark and challenge another day!

I guess no one understands what it's like for us Pomeranians, big hearts and even bigger egos trapped in tiny fanciful bodies who just can't accept being downgraded from our larger, more powerful Chow Chow ancestors to a toy breed. Even the name "toy" breed is derogatory! Most of us refuse to face the reality of our size and our limitations and think we are gung-ho enough to take on any dog, the bigger, the greater the challenge!

I am the worst of the lot; I can't stand the sight of any other dog walking this planet! The moment I see any dog, no matter what breed and what size, it just drives me mad and I just have to get at the poor animal and run it off the earth!

"I don't know why you are so cantankerous and hate everybody, Eric?" Jennifer would lament. "Why don't you just relax and make friends with some of the dogs at the park? You may find out that you can have a good time with them!"

But I didn't agree and would have none of it.

Once she tried to bring me to a kind of dog gathering that her club of snooty dog lovers held once a month.

"It'll be good for you to learn some socializing skills and you'll see that you can have lots of fun with the other dogs," she assured me as she brushed my fur out to its full Pomeranian potential and bundled me into the car for the ride to the event.

I tried to warn her that she was making a big mistake taking me there because I just have an irresistible impulse to savage any dog I see; and the day would end with the two of us slinking off with our tails between our legs. But she wouldn't listen. I was at my prime and looking absolutely gorgeous and she wanted to show me off to everyone at the dog club.

"No sense in having such a beautiful dog and hiding him at home everyday just because he has a bit of an attitude problem," she told Tanya who knew my lack of respect for class and society much better than her mother did and wisely opted to stay away!

"Are you sure you want to do this, Mom?" Tanya asked as she helped Jennifer put me into my best collar and leash. "You know what he's like with other dogs and for the record, I wouldn't say that he has 'just a bit' of an attitude problem!"

"Well, if we don't try, we will never know, will we?" Jennifer retorted, bravely determined.

I glared at her. I really didn't want to go because I hated the sound and smell of other dogs, and I am totally, absolutely and incurably anti-social. Why wouldn't she just accept that?

Then my eyes started to shine with a wicked glint and I thought, "All right, madam, if you insist, I will go and take all those holier than thou creatures down! Here I come, Eric to the battlefield!"

Every mother believes her child is an angel incarnate and Jennifer was no different. Despite being tested over and over again, she still thought I was the world's most gorgeous, most lovable and most irresistible dog! By the end of that day at the dog show, I'm sure she was the only one who thought so!

If dogs could have headaches, I think I had one by the time we arrived at the large open space shaded by tall spreading trees which was teeming with dogs of all shapes and sizes. God, there must be dozens of them and I had never seen such a large gathering of canines but what were they? Real angels from heaven or robotic dogs? How did they sit so quietly in rows each with his or her owner behind holding on to fanciful leashes (bought to outdo each other at the event, I am sure of that)?

All heads turned as we made a grand and unruly entry into this arena of well-bred, lofty dogs, with me straining vigorously on a comparatively unremarkable leash that Jennifer was trying to hold on to for all she was worth.

"Here, Eric, here is our slot and please behave, don't embarrass Mommy!" she hissed, pressing me to a spot beside a disdainful poodle. First mistake of the day! I couldn't stand the supercilious poodle with her ridiculous bunches of bobbing curls which just drove me up the wall. I am a thoroughly undisciplined dog wholly driven by instinct and (this I'm ashamed to admit), wickedness. The more cross I am, the meaner I get and I was really mad to be forced into this show for nitwits! And now I was being put next to this holier than thou specimen they called a dog!

I tried to hold myself down chanting the words over and over again like a mantra that I had to behave for Jennifer's sake, because having people at the dog club admire and respect us was so important to her! I succeeded for exactly five minutes and then the bobbing curls and huge pink bows got the better of me and to my horror, the next I knew I had flung myself on a poodle, tearing viciously at her curls and pulling the offending pink bows loose. All hell broke loose as the poodle let out a howl that just went on and on, provoking the other dogs to abandon their sentry-like positions and roll all over each other. A cloud of clips, ribbons and dog accessories also went flying.

Jennifer stood frozen with horror at what I had started for just a few seconds before she rushed over and yanked me off the poodle, apologizing profusely to her owner. Far from being repentant for my crime, I laughed and laughed at the sight of the poodle, for all of her carefully coiffed curls now were standing on end as if put through a washing machine at high spin.

She was furious and she hissed into my ears, "You bad, bad boy! And wipe that irritating grin off your face! Look at what you've done! Causing a pandemonium like that. I'm ashamed of you!"

I realized that she was really, really mad and I had done it this time so it was far better to tow the line and look repentant than to take the defiant route. I did what I knew would steal her heart, licking her furiously in the face, but she didn't buy it this time. She threw me down on the ground real hard so I went into Plan B, immediately rolling over and pleading with my eyes, "Yes, I've been bad, very bad and I deserve any punishment you hand out to me. See, total submission, just punish me any way you think fit. I'm at your mercy."

Of course, Jennifer softened but she had to save face by showing her displeasure with me. She pulled me over to Mink, the poodle, and said, "See, Mink, Eric is very sorry for what he did. He knows he is a very bad boy!"

"Mink! What a name!" I thought contemptuously and, although I was still in my submissive position, Mink could see the wicked gleam in my half-closed eyes and she ran to her owner, whining about my evilness and how "not sorry" I was. Thankfully, no one but me could understand what she was trying to say!

Jennifer had had it with me and wanted to take me off the

show and back home. But Mink's owner graciously insisted I should stay, or perhaps she wanted to give us more opportunities to show the whole dog community what a low-class, badly brought up dog I was. And we fell headlong into that trap!

Eventually, they managed to get all the dogs calmed down and back in their places. They put me right at the front presumably so that I could be watched and prevented from creating more mischief. I had to admit grudgingly that all the dogs were extremely well mannered and for the first time, I asked myself why I couldn't be more like them so that Jennifer would be happy.

But I'd done enough damage for the day and I knew that if I created any more mischief, Jennifer would really get mad and no amount of pleading or buttering her up would do any good. So with a supreme effort, I forced myself to stay put on my haunches, controlling my urge to get up by tapping one of my paws ever so softly so that no one would notice.

Someone was making an announcement that the next event was the listening and obeying commands exercise. Jennifer looked really nervous now because she knew that I hadn't the slightest respect for commands and did exactly what I wanted. In fact, far from obeying, I was very likely to do just the opposite.

I caught her eye and tried to reassure her that it was different this time, I would try my best to do whatever they asked me, for her sake, but she didn't look very convinced. I sighed. It was terrible not to be trusted but, well, could anyone blame her? I would just have to show her then.

I started out with really good intentions but they were putting out bowls of food in front of each dog and what kind of dog food was it that could smell so good? We were supposed to control our instinctive desire to immediately eat up the food in front of us till we were given the command to start; that was one of the obeying commands exercises. Well-mannered and well-bred dogs were supposed to be able to control basic animal instincts and wait.

Later I would insist that they were all out to sabotage me and show me up because I had never seen any dog food that smelled so good! It was my undoing and before I even realized what I was doing, I had already walloped up the food in my bowl and was steadily going through the bowls of all the other dogs, overturning some in the process! Poor Jennifer! She looked ready to collapse with mortification as she sprang into action and scooped me up from the fifth bowl I was starting to attack.

This time, she was determined to call it quits and accept that I was untrainable and would never be civilized and anyway, no one invited us to stay for the rest of the show as Jennifer picked up our things and raced to the car with flaming cheeks. She nagged me the whole journey back and even called me names.

I really got an earful this time and had to sit through it without daring to make a sound because when Jennifer was this mad, that was the wisest thing to do. She refused to talk to me or even look in my direction for the rest of the day and it was fortunate that I had stolen enough food from the other dogs to be able to go without any dinner or snacks that night.

A week later, a friend remarked how perfect my posture and markings were and urged Jennifer to enter me for the Kennel Club Dog Show.

The whole family replied in horrified unison, "No, no and no!"

So that was the end of my short-lived dog show career. Bill's efforts to breed champion bloodline into me were all in vain!

CHAPTER | Ten

In case you think so, I am actually even fifteen pounds of brawn, thug and self-indulgent nastiness. Even I do have my moments of tenderness especially for my Mom, Jennifer. And everyone in the family agrees that it's usually in the calm euphoric moments of bedtime when I am the sweetest!

During the day, I may be all macho but come night, I become vulnerable because I have a secret phobia: I'm terrified of the dark and sleeping alone! I just can't help that and although I've tried to overcome it, I just can't.

Jennifer could have used that against me if she wanted to, but bless her soul, she never did capitalize on my weaknesses, not even on the night of that dreadful Dog Club show fiasco when I dragged her to hell and back. She just banished me to the far end of the bed and refused to give me her usual goodnight cuddle and, knowing that she needed space, I stayed away from her. But I was so down and sad that I went straight to sleep without my habitual bedtime "fussing around," rolling on the bed and pawing at the bedspread and bed sheets to mess it up.

I don't like to sleep in the open, especially at night because I have this fear of being attacked by predatory and dangerous elements. I need to burrow myself into some covered space to feel protected. That is why I mess up the bedspread to create a kind of hole to crawl into and be "protected."

My other mother, Tracy, always kept us close to her and

warned us about venturing too far out by ourselves in the open fields because one never knew when there were foxes and birds of prey lurking around to nab plump, defenseless puppies like us. At night, she slept with us firmly tucked in her paws. The thought of her made me very blue that night. Yes, I still think of Tracy and sometimes I miss her although I know there is no use yearning for her because I will never see her again. I don't even know whether she still remembers me. Probably not, because she must have had other puppies after us.

So who says dogs are not emotional or smart enough to remember people, incidents and habits acquired from another world? Take it back, whoever said that! I, for one, remember all of them—Tracy, Bill, Sue and the huge sprawling farm that looked like the whole world to me then. They sometimes appear in my dreams and that's why you see me laughing, crying, twitching and sighing deeply in my sleep! Recently I think a lot about Sue because Tanya has distanced herself from me and hardly plays with me anymore. I miss having a playmate to horse around with. Jennifer tries her best but, you know, she's a Mom so it's not the same, "horsing" with your Mom.

But I now live in a city and the only jungles are concrete and the only animals and birds of prey are in the zoo or kept as domestic pets so I don't have anything to fear at all in the safety of my own apartment. And yet, the old habits, illusions and fears die hard and I simply haven't been able to shake them off. I don't think I ever will.

It may surprise you because I am so gregarious and hyperactive but sometimes even I need my own space and quiet moments. Our apartment is quite spacious but by no means palatial. It's a typical three-bedroom home so it's not easy to find an untouched corner where no one can find me for more than thirty minutes at a stretch.

One day, however, quite by chance, I stumbled upon the perfect spot. Tanya has a four-poster bed in her room with a bed skirt that covers up the space under the bed and Jennifer uses that space to store the extra bed sheets and blankets in soft plastic cases and bags. That day, a toy I was playing with rolled under the bed and I crawled in to retrieve it and didn't emerge for two hours! I had found a cool, dim nest among the soft bags of blankets and bed sheets under the bed that was curtained off from the rest of the apartment and no one could bother me there. Even if John, Jennifer or Tanya found out I was there, they wouldn't be able to reach inside and drag me out because they all know that when disturbed, I can become hostile and snap instinctively. So they would still have to leave me to come out voluntarily by myself. It was just the perfect place for me to escape and find some peace!

I called it my "nest" and it was a wonderful secret hideout that I could disappear into when I wanted to be alone without someone always around to pat me, talk to me or bother me one way or the other. Sometimes dogs can be stressed out too by all the attention and it's worse for us because we can't, say, take a vacation, or watch a movie, or do something to de-stress. We can't go anywhere ourselves and must always wait for someone to take us. Can you see how stressful this can get, total dependence on our masters' goodwill? I guess this is why I am so defiant, fighting against the system, you might say. Thankfully I have very tolerant and loving owners who put up with all my idiosyncrasies and love me for what I am!

The first time I disappeared into my "nest," when Jennifer came back and couldn't find me, she panicked, searching the whole house for me and I heard her calling John almost in tears, "I can't find Eric. Is it possible he somehow managed to get out of the house? But how? I'm absolutely sure when I left this morning, he did his song and dance thing and I threw him a snack and locked the door! So he has to be somewhere around the house but I've searched everywhere!"

I knew I should just come out and put an end to my poor Mom's agony but my nest was so cozy and I was so relaxed that I just refused to budge, not even for love of Jennifer.

Then she got the better of me because she knew exactly what would get me. The keys! Jennifer knows that I can never ever resist the sound of keys jingling because that means someone is leaving the house.

As she fully expected, the minute I heard the tantalizing jingling of the keys, taunting the complacence out of me, the familiar surge of energy rushed into my system, destroying my peace and tranquility of the last two hours. I tried to resist the urge to get up and rush to the door but it was impossible, I am but a slave to my own instincts!

But I didn't want to let her know my hiding place so I crept out as quietly as possible and gathered speed only outside the room. I flung myself at Jennifer in full song and dance display, turning round and round till I was dizzy and breathless. I think I gave an extra vigorous rendition of what John calls my "parting shots" because I felt a little guilty but for once she didn't mind. My Mom was just so glad to know that I was safe and sound in the house and not wandering around somewhere outside, lost and homeless.

I heard her telling John once that she was so afraid I would get lost because if that happened, she was sure no one would take me in because of my attitude problem and my unmanageable eccentricities. I agreed wholeheartedly with her and made a mental note never to get lost and become homeless.

"Oh Eric, you naughty boy," she shouted above the din. "Didn't you hear me calling? Where were you? Come on; show

Mommy where you came from!"

But I refused to oblige and slyly distracted her from insisting on an answer by giving her a magnificent display of affection. I knew she would find out soon enough but until that happened; I really wanted to hang on to my secret nest for as long as possible. It felt really nice and well, private, having my own little place that no one knew about. It also became the place where I hid all the things I stole from the house, be it a piece of lingerie I refused to return or one of Tanya's soft, squishy soft toys or brightly colored socks.

I love my family to bits and can't imagine getting by a single day without seeing them but they never really leave me alone when they're home. I wouldn't be able to count the number of times in the course of a day that one or other of them scoops me up and rain kisses and hugs on me and my every wish is their command—especially Jennifer. Usually, I lap all that attention up with great pleasure, enjoying every moment of it but there are also times when I am in one of my aloof moods and find all that babying too cloying but no one cares what mood I am in, they literally smother me with love and expect me to be always ready for it! They don't seem to understand that even for dogs, there can be too much of a good thing!

Jennifer even keeps a packet of my favorite snacks ever ready beside her computer so that she can satisfy my demand for a bite any time! She thinks it's obscene to make me wait! They even give me a nickname, VID, Very Important Dog!

So much pampering, so much love and overindulgence, who am I to complain? I haven't been seriously disciplined since the day I stepped into this house and yet, sometimes I dream of being given just one day where I can get away from this concrete jungle and feel the wind in my face as I race through open fields of wild flowers and springy grass, free of supervision and the restraint of a leash.

But as the saying goes, "you can't have your cake and eat it" so we trade freedom and the right to choose for all the comforts of a warm, loving family and home and life outside on a leash.

All these thoughts are going through my mind in those moments when I lie quietly on the cool marble floor, face between my paws in what Jennifer calls "my pensive" and "reflective" mode.

CHAPTER | *Eleven*

Recently Jennifer became very health and exercise conscious so she started renting a bicycle in the East Coast Park, an esplanade by the sea with a narrow stretch of beach. I just love this place and its rows of beach clubs, pubs and cafes by the sea. There are lots of young people rollerblading or wind surfing in the sea and music from the beach clubs and the little market nearby make the whole place very gay with a kind of party atmosphere especially on weekends.

I'd never been to a beach and the first time I felt my paws sinking into the soft grainy sands I was almost delirious with excitement. My nostrils literally flared open to take in the salt-tinged air the sea winds brought in, and the gently rolling waves lapping against the shoreline was the closest to Nature I had ever been on this concrete island I now call home. I fell in love with the sea, the beach and the swaying palm trees and if Jennifer doesn't take me there at least once a fortnight, I don't give her peace.

Sometimes when she's real busy, she sighs and says she wishes she hadn't introduced me to the beach but I know she doesn't really mean it! Something I notice about humans, they say a lot of things they don't really mean and sometimes, it sends out the wrong signals. Fortunately I know Jennifer so well I can always tell when she's serious about what she says and when she's not!

The East Coast Park, which is what that stretch of beach is called, is a very dog-friendly place and a small area is cordoned off for dog shows almost every weekend but Jennifer and I steer clear of them. We might hang around the edge of the crowds to watch the dogs parading on the stage and showing off their skills but never to participate for very obvious reasons! Although my papers declare me of champion and show dog lineage, my whole family has accepted that I will never be one myself.

But I know they don't care about that and still love me for what I am. I have heard plenty of stories about the families who buy a pedigree dog just as a status symbol and force them into dog shows no matter what and I'm so glad my family got me to bring love and joy into their lives, for better and a lot of the times, for worse!

Sometimes, just for a lark, I emit my special edition gunfire spray of sharp piercing barks intended to destabilize the "cat walking" dogs on stage and they usually do. Jennifer bundles me quickly away before the irate owners track us down but I can tell by the faint smile on her face that she is also enjoying it.

When she takes off on her bicycle, Jennifer puts me in the mesh wire basket strapped to the front. As we gather speed, a cool breeze springs up and it's lifting the fur from my face, higher and higher, and I feel as if I'm flying! It's wonderful and liberating, and I shriek at Jennifer, why did we wait so long to do this?

We usually cycle along the designated cycling path for at least an hour, stopping at a rocky outcrop to watch the tropical sun slowly setting into the sea. The sky fills with a rainbow of orange, red and yellow streaks and it's breathtakingly beautiful! We wait till the last rays of sun have disappeared into the horizon before cycling slowly back to the bicycle rental shop.

And after we return the bicycle, Jennifer and I flop down on one of the stone benches on the esplanade, waiting for the lights of the ships to come alive and then we soak in the brilliance of those twinkling lights, little diamonds lighting up the darkening sea and sky. There we are, mistress and dog, sitting side by side, our silhouettes etched against the darkening sky, in perfect harmony. It's an awesome union of hearts, minds and souls!

Up in the sky, planes are taking off and landing in the airport nearby and their faint drone jolts my memory of a time when perhaps I was in one of those metal birds, being flown to a distant land and an uncertain life.

It is rush hour at the airport and the sky is filled with planes, circling to take off or land and we sit watching them quietly for a while. After sometime I start to pant vigorously because the breeze has stopped fanning us and the humid tropical night is eating into my two layers of fur.

Jennifer gets up and says the welcome words, "Come on, let's go get a cold drink with lots and lots of ice!"

A lady comes up to us and says, "What a beautiful dog but you should keep his fur longer!"

I glare at her and spit, "Yes, try wearing a fur coat in a sauna and let's see how beautiful you feel!"

She doesn't understand what I said and draws back, commenting nervously, "But he's not very friendly, is he?"

These people just don't know how a dog feels, weighed down by two layers of insulating fur in the tropical heat; thank God Jennifer isn't like that! She always takes me to Danny's to shear off my golden locks when I look too weighed down and there's a heat wave hitting us.

Sometimes he overdoes it and I end up with a funny crew cut which makes me feel naked and small and for the first week, I avoid looking at myself in the mirror because I know I don't look good. But did I feel light with all that load of fur taken off me!

It's a chicken and egg kind of thing actually. I know I look absolutely gorgeous with my full Pomeranian coat but I get so hot and overloaded with fur in the humid tropical sizzle that I can hardly breathe and spend most of my time just flopping on any cool surface, panting. So it's a choice between beauty or cool comfort and having a life and of course I chose the latter. So sometimes, when Jennifer is too busy and forgets to take me to Danny's on time, I make sure I let her know!

But heat or no heat, I love going out and can literally go mad if I don't get out of the house at least once a day. My favorite spots are a couple of local coffee shops where dogs are welcomed and I am accorded all the courtesies of a "regular." The proprietors know my family goes there once or sometimes twice a day because of me so they treat me really well. Jennifer can't bear to leave me behind so the family has to eat at one of only three open air restaurants where dogs are welcomed. That's how much they indulge me! So I am treated like a VID at those places, holding court and enjoying every minute of it!

Two weeks ago, I had a hair-raising experience, and well, I probably deserved it! Tanya had taken me for a walk and I was mad with her because she refused to carry me and I had to walk. The rough gravel on the road hurt my paws and I struggled with the leash to get her attention but she was too engrossed with the favorite pastime of teens these days—texting her friends on her cell phone—to notice.

Jennifer had bathed me earlier in the afternoon and somehow fixed my collar on too loose and with a final twist, I managed to slip out of it to escape Tanya and headed off down the road. I'd just go and disappear for a while and teach that missy a lesson, I thought as I continued running. I was so engrossed on punishing Tanya that I didn't notice where I was actually running to!

She realized almost immediately that I was missing when the

leash felt weightless and came running after me, screaming frantically for me to come back and that made me dash even faster. I didn't realize I had run blindly into the road until I saw a car heading towards me. For a moment I froze and thought I'd had it and I could see my obituary flashing by me, "Eric, male Pomeranian, dead, aged four years. Cause of death, foolhardiness."

No, no, I'm too young to die! I screamed, and lay down on the road, flattening myself as much as I could, in the way that I had seen cats do to get under a narrow gap. Then I closed my eyes waiting for either the car to roll over me, taking me along in a deadly crashing of bones, fur and flesh; or clearing safely over me. Whichever way it went, I deserved what I got; I had to learn to be less self-indulgent and to tone down that huge ego and the tendency to cut off my nose to spite my face.

I held my breath as a terrific whirring of dust, petrol fumes, burning air and an ominous dark shadow rolled over me followed by two others till the traffic lights behind turned red and the flow of vehicles stopped at last.

It was only when the air above me cleared that I realized the stream of cars had stopped and somehow I was still alive. I scrambled to my feet and raced to the pavement guided by the sound of Tanya's voice screaming to me to "Hurry, Eric! Hurry!"

I cleared the road just as the traffic lights turned green and the roar of scores of vehicles of all sizes started up again and thundered towards me like an army of deadly soldiers.

Tanya scooped me into her arms and hugged me tightly; she had never seen me so humbled and shaken before which was understandable considering that I had just survived three vehicles rolling over me at top speed on a busy trunk road! When the vehicles cleared, she had expected to see me flattened to a bloody pulp and the sight of me bouncing back large as life made her hysterical with joy. We forgot the past year when she had practically ignored me and we had drifted apart as she became preoccupied with the difficulties of being a teen in turbulent times and I got left behind in her world because I was, well, just the family dog.

I was none the worse for wear and except for a line of singed fur down my back where I had been scorched by the hot exhaust fumes of the vehicles thundering over me and a lungful of foul air, I had escaped, unscathed. It was a miracle that a bad dog like me didn't deserve and I felt humbled by it, at least, for the rest of that day!

"Bad boy! Don't ever do that again, do you hear?" Tanya shrieked angrily at me and when she gets mad, her voice can be really shrill, enough to split the ear! But I knew she was mad this time simply because she was so relieved and she even carried me home the rest of the way and didn't trust herself to put me down.

After that incident, we drew closer again because I think Tanya realized how close she had been to losing me and on my part, too, I learned never to take life so carelessly for granted.

We made a pact on the way home not to tell Jennifer because if we did, she might never allow Tanya to take me out alone again. But we can never hide anything from Jennifer for long; she always finds out in the end!

She took me to task of course for what I did and warned me, "I know you think you are like a cat with nine lives but you've already used up most of those lives so my advice to you, Eric, is, watch it!"

I gave her one of my angelic looks but I was growling under my breath, "Hey, stop nagging will you, woman? I've used up only four lives at last count so I've still got five left to gamble with!"

Jennifer mistook my subdued little growls for apologies and

patted me, "I know you're sorry, Eric and I forgive you but I'm just so afraid something will happen to you if you continue this reckless life style of dashing into busy traffic and challenging dogs three or four times your size!"

God, how dense humans can be sometimes but if it makes them happy to think we are saying what they want to hear, so be it. After all, it's always better for us to keep our masters happy than mad at us!

There are definite benefits to making Jennifer happy but I also give a lot of love in return especially when she is down. I instinctively know her moods and when she is really blue and sad, her feelings flow into me and I feel, really feel for her; such is the bond between us.

At such times, I stop all my shenanigans and just sit very close to her and let her know I am there, a warm, breathing, living creature who will never betray her and sometimes, if I feel it will do her good, I nuzzle her in the ribs till she breaks out into fits of giggles and well, you know, there is a lot of truth in the saying "Laughter is the best medicine."

I am just a dog and a tiny one at that so I can't do much for my family but I sometimes hear Jennifer tell her friends, "I'm so glad I have Eric and even though he's quite a handful, believe it or not, stroking his fur has a calming effect on me! He is my stresser and destresser at the same time!"

Hearing those words makes me feel so proud and useful because I feel that in some small way, I have made a difference in Jennifer's life. Maybe our masters never look at it this way, but even dogs like to feel useful and needed. That's why I am so obsessed with protecting our home; I feel that I have a duty to prevent anyone from coming to our home and touching my family's things. It's one of the few ways I can repay my family for all the love and care they lavish so unconditionally on me.

John and Jennifer have tried to explain to me over and over again that our visitors are friends who are invited to come to the house and they will never harm us but I refuse to listen to them. I am determined that as long as there is breath in my body, I will try to keep everyone away so that no harm will ever come to my family. I can't accept that what I'm doing is giving my parents and Tanya more problems and embarrassment than protection and when I make up my mind on something, it's near impossible to convince me otherwise!

I hate it when anyone touches anyone especially Jennifer because I think of her as a woman who needs a man's protection—no matter that in this case, the "man" is hardly two feet tall and weighs less than fifteen pounds! Once, the postman came to deliver a parcel and as he approached Jennifer to ask for her signature. I thought he was trying to attack her. Furious, I flung myself at him and sank my teeth into his ankle. Fortunately, he was wearing boots so my teeth didn't draw sufficient blood for him to threaten my family with a lawsuit!

When the ruckus had died down, Jennifer told me she was grateful for my loyalty and good intentions to protect her but could I just stick to growling in the future? I shook my head vigorously, no; growling was not enough from someone as small as me.

"When you are as small as me, more drastic and aggressive action is needed," I protested. "That's why I strut around and use my teeth so much, to give the effect of power and aggression."

"What about growling and dancing around and snapping but not touching 'the enemy'?" she asked.

I thought about that and we finally agreed on dancing, just short of touching ,as a scare tactic only and that way, no blood is drawn, no one gets hurt and my family doesn't live in fear of lawsuits!

CHAPTER Twelve

"I'm *sure Eric took it but* he won't be able to recall where he put it. Remember, he's just a dog!"

"Dogs can't recognize more than a few words so it's no point confusing him!"

These are assumptions that really irk me. What do people mean by "just a dog?" God gave us brains (granted, some smaller than others) to think, remember and do things, and hearts to feel and to love, so yes, I can remember that piece of soap I stole from Jennifer's bathroom. It hasn't surfaced simply because I refuse to surrender it; the smell is too good and I have it safely hidden in my "nest."

No one knows it but a lot of "missing" things are hidden in my "nest." I'm a hopeless kleptomaniac of sweet smelling things, from any perfume bottles within my reach, to scented soaps, Jennifer's aromatherapy sachets and even Tanya's fancy erasers and note paper that I manage to filch from time to time. There's a wealth of such goodies in my nest. I seldom touch John's things except for the occasional pair of socks because they are boring, unimaginative and have neither color nor smell to attract a kleptomaniac dog.

Jennifer doesn't know why I have that worried look on my face whenever she goes near Tanya's bed but I'm terrified she will discover my loot and confiscate all of it! But so far it hasn't happened yet and sometimes I suspect she knows but prefers to let sleeping dogs lie, so to speak, because she guesses how important my "personal space" is to me!

It's John I'm afraid of because he has no respect for or emotions about stuff like "personal spaces" of a dog and will quite happily raid my nest of loot if he finds out what I've been up to! Sometimes he can be quite insensitive and, in a typical guy fashion, he believes that any dog that has a good home and family can't complain or need anything more.

So to every member of my family who accuses me of not being able to remember where I keep the things I pilfer because I am just a dog, it's not that I am too stupid to remember but that I refuse to return them. Do you know what, I think I outsmart them more times than they know!

The people who live with me know that I have a very short fuse and I don't need a lot of provocation to get angry. I know I should be more tolerant and it's bad for the heart to get worked up all the time but I can't help it and from the age of three years, I have had to take a medication for my weak heart, a quarter tablet that Jennifer has to coax or bribe down my throat every single day for the rest of my life!

I heard Tanya and Jennifer talk about a "staring" incident where two boys got into a bloody fight because one of them objected to the other staring at him and it's a guy kind of thing. I remember thinking how strange that we male dogs also hate being stared at and just a few minutes of staring is enough to get our hackles up. Guys will be guys and male dogs and male humans do share some common animal instincts after all!

Sometimes Tanya and even Jennifer try to provoke me deliberately by staring. I know it and I try not to give them the satisfaction of seeing me lose my cool but I can't. I just can't hold out for long because if there's one thing I hate most, it's being stared at.

I hold back for just ten seconds then the low growl at the

base of my throat becomes louder and before I know it, I am emitting these short, piercing angry barks and going round in circles to express my displeasure.

Jennifer or Tanya, depending on who was doing the staring, would catch me in mid-spin and say soothingly, "Okay, okay, Eric, it was just a joke! Don't you have a sense of humor?"

Another thing that gets me mad is when they play this give and retrieve trick on me, holding out a piece of snack to me and then snatching it back before I can pick it up. They think it's funny and entertaining but I find it downright insulting! Okay, I normally put up with this good naturedly for two or three times but when they repeat it a fourth time, I feel I am entitled to lose my cool and snap at them to stop teasing me!

"Hey, don't you know it's not nice to tease a poor dog out of whatever little dignity he has?"

They know by the tone of my barking that they have gone too far and toss me the snack which promptly soothes my ruffled feathers and all is forgiven although not forgotten!

I can be cunning, shrewd and drive a hard bargain sometimes to get what I want. There are days when even Jennifer will not give me a snack, declaring me too fat. When I get really mad or desperate or both, I will go to Jennifer's lingerie bag which I can reach if I stand up on my hind legs. I hunt around for her favorite silk stockings and bring it up to her, firmly gripped in my mouth and threaten to tear them up.

She watches me with her heart in her mouth but she knows I will not return them to her without anything in exchange so with eyes begging me to be careful with her stockings, she reaches out for the snack box and says, "Here, Eric, let's make a deal, you give me the stockings in exchange for this snack. How about that?"

It suited me fine because that was exactly what I wanted and I wait till she places the snack within my reach before I drop the stockings. I know it's mean but sometimes it's the only way to get what I want!

Sometimes, I will go for coins because I know Jennifer and John are terrified when they see me with a coin in my mouth; they are so afraid I will swallow it and hurt myself. But of course, I'm not that stupid, I have no intention of swallowing it and if they look closely, they will see that I make sure I grip the coin with my teeth just inside my mouth so I can spit it out anytime but they don't know and they think I might swallow the coin if they don't give in to me and "exchange" for a snack.

But they may have a point: I'm taking a risk here because accidents can happen and just a slip up on my grip could indeed send the coin slithering down my throat and then it could be a long wait for it to be passed out or I would need a painful and expensive surgery to remove it!

"Who says dogs can't do business?" Jennifer laughs when she has safely retrieved her precious silk stockings or sometimes a coin or once even a pair of scissors! "Just see what a hard bargain this one drives!"

There's another thing I can't stand and that is injustice, especially when I am wrongly accused of something I didn't do, that really gets me! Take the time Tanya went through a phase when she would blame me for everything that went wrong if she could get away with it but most of the time I didn't let her do that. Just because I couldn't talk didn't mean I couldn't defend myself by some means or other.

If, for instance, anything was found missing or broken, she would say "It must be Eric who did that! Bad boy!"

I didn't see why I should be labeled "Bad boy" if I didn't deserve it so I would march up to Jennifer and bark my innocence, refusing to stop till she accepted my version and forced a confession out of Tanya.

Although I still love Tanya because, well, she is family, after all, I lost a bit of respect for her after a spate of such "tell tale" and sneaky incidents. I was resentful because, look, Tanya is a human, given a tongue and speech to speak for herself, she should know better than try to make a poor, defenseless dog who speaks a language no one understands take flack for her misdeeds!

But Jennifer knows that I am a dog of integrity and if I did anything wrong, I always accept responsibility for it. If she came home, for example, and found me sitting quietly in a corner, my eyes two dark pools of guilt, or hiding behind the stereo speakers, eyes narrowed to worried slits, she would know straight away that I had broken some heinous house rule or other. She would make a big show of searching everywhere for evidence of my misdemeanor and when she found it, she would circle round it a few times and call out "Eric, come here!"

It was punishment time and I knew I had to take it like a man so I would approach her slowly, almost crawling on all fours and when I reached her, I would roll over on my back, four legs in the air and wait for the inevitable.

This is what she calls my "surrender" and "do whatever you need to do with me" mode and this posture of abject regret and apology never fails to soften her and John. Most of the time, I get away with a couple of light spanks on the hind legs and a warning.

They know there is no need to spank hard and hurt me so most of the time it's just light to medium size smacks unless it's a really very serious offence. For me, the humiliation and "loss of face" of being spanked and having Tanya smirking, is enough punishment.

Sometimes my Mom would be too tired to discipline me even though I am ready and waiting and then she'd just walk past the crime scene pretending not to notice anything because if she saw it, she'd have to punish me or lose my respect. I'd wait, hardly able to believe that I'd got away with blue murder but although I was officially reprieved, I'd still be cautious around her for a while!

Sometimes Tanya would spoil it all by protesting, "Eric did something wrong and he's hiding in the corner! Aren't you going to punish him?"

Jennifer would glare at her, giving her the "Please shut up. I'm too tired to deal with him today so I'm just not going to notice it" look. She thinks I didn't see that look but I did and somehow, it makes me more remorseful than an official punishment because I knew I'd upset my Mom and forced her to "deal" with me even though she was so tired.

And it doesn't help that sometimes Tanya can be a real pain in the neck, throwing tantrums befitting a prima dona! I'm beginning to dislike her and just don't see why she can't give Jennifer a break from all her moods and "being difficult," even I am trying! I'm thinking teenage dogs are a whole lot nicer than teenage girls and boys! No wonder Jennifer and John call me the "Stress Reliever!"

Tanya and I are definitely going through a period of "sibling rivalry" and yet she won't do anything to endear herself to her parents the way I do and then grouses about it when I get more attention than her!

John is quite superstitious and he is convinced that I am his good luck mascot! I heard him telling Jennifer that whenever he pats my "good luck" head before leaving to attend to a big deal, it always goes through! One day, he came back, dejected, and swore that because he had forgotten to give me his customary pat on the head, his deal had fallen apart!

I really don't know whether I should believe in my own good luck charms or not but one doesn't play with spiritual things. In any case, I am always happy to be of service to my family!

CHAPTER | *Thirteen*

Even dogs have the occasional fetish, I know I have a couple, one of which I am not particularly proud of but just cannot help myself. I love ladies lingerie and used to raid Jennifer and Tanya's underwear basket till they got so fed they kept their intimate wear hidden deep inside tightly closed wardrobes and away from prying dogs with disgusting fetishes!

Even then, I watch and wait for the times they accidentally drop a bra, panty or stockings or forget their lingerie-napping dog and carelessly drape the stuff over a chair and within seconds, I have whisked the garments off to some secluded corner or my nest to chew and play with. Some of Jennifer's stuff are pure silk and very expensive and she throws a fit when she can't find them. Sometimes I feel sorry for her so I return the expensive pieces after I'm through with them.

There's something about the soft, silky feel of ladies' underwear especially Jennifer's I just can't resist, the more flimsy the happier I am! But I know my Mom and Tanya need those things and they are really expensive so I am always careful never to tear them, except by accident.

My Mom just can't understand why I demean myself by stealing underwear, and brave being labeled "Pervert!" and described as a gross, disgusting dog! Sometimes I try to control myself because, well, pervert isn't a very nice reputation to be stuck with but the minute I see a panty, bra or stockings lying around, I'm lost and all good intentions are thrown to the wind! I guess maybe I am as gross as they say! But someday, when I'm older and wiser, I must get rid of this habit! But for the moment, just let me make use of the fallacies of youth to enjoy it!

There's a funny side or a twist to this whole lingerie hijacking thing, depending on how you want to look at it. Sometimes, if Jennifer forgets to pick up after my philandering ways, an unexpected visitor might find a trail of panties or bra in the living room or stuffed behind the cushions on the couch or under the coffee table. It's terribly embarrassing when this happens and Jennifer gamely tries to laugh it off by explaining to her amused guests her dog, Eric's fascination with ladies' underwear. I don't know whether they believe that or not but at least everyone has a good laugh over it!

One day, my family had a debate on whether the "pervert" in their midst only had eyes for ladies lingerie or whether he was also attracted to men's underwear. So they decided to test me out by leaving a couple of John's briefs lying around but I wasn't in the least interested. Men's underwear is so rough and unimaginative and well, downright ugly and shapeless, which dog in his right mind would go for that stuff! They got the message and declared me not only a pervert but definitely a "ladies' man" as well!

"Look, Mom, Eric is blushing!" Tanya screamed with delight and she was right.

Whenever I'm embarrassed, the inside of my ears turn a bright pink and I feel my whole face go hot so yes, I guess you can call that blushing. After all, with my face all covered in fur, the only way you can tell I'm blushing is the reddening of the insides of my ears!

Another disgusting habit I have is to go through every trash can in the house. I am thoroughly ashamed and humiliated by what Jennifer said "a classy, smart dog like Eric" shouldn't do! She is right of course, I have no business to be digging up trash when I sleep on a nice bed in air conditioned comfort and am hand-fed on food and snacks air flown from Japan! But what do you know, everyone including dogs, do have their trashy side!

I may be all fussy about the newspapers in my toilet corner being changed every time I use it but the minute I see a trash can, I am lost! Jennifer gave up trying to talk me out of this disgusting habit and got so tired of picking up after every toppled trash can in the house that eventually, she put away all the trash cans into storage. Now plastic bags hanging well out of my reach serve as the family's trash receptacles and my scavenging days are over!

My Mom grumbled a lot at first that our apartment looked so untidy and "uncivilized" with plastic bags hanging all over and lamented that all the beautiful chrome trash cans she had bought now graced only the store room. But eventually, the whole family had to get used to plastic bags hanging on almost every door knob in our apartment, thanks to me!

"But at least there's nothing else left for him to scavenge," Jennifer said although she should know me better than that!

One gray rainy day, when I was left alone in the house almost the whole day and got really bored and a little resentful at the way I was being "neglected," I discovered the excitement of digging into the laundry basket, much to poor Jennifer's horror. She got real mad when she returned home to see the basket over turned and dirty clothes strewn all over the utility yard and couldn't understand why I did that. Hanging up plastic bags for trash was one thing but hanging up the laundry basket?

"Eric!" she sighed. "Everyday you think of new ways to cause havoc in this house! Why can't you be more like Aunt Meri's dog, Scarlet or at least, just try to be a little bit more, you know, normal?"

How do I explain to her that the clothes in the laundry basket contain all the smells of my family, my Mom, my Dad and Tanya that I love? These smells are special and make me feel all warm and safe and nice inside. Most of all, they remind me of the smell of my other mother, Tracy, in the farm, whom everyone thinks I have forgotten but I haven't.

Tanya, of course, is the usual town crier of my misdeeds with her yells of, "Eric's in the laundry basket again!"

Really, I wonder how a sweet loving child managed to become so mean! If she were not family, I would write her off. Jennifer doesn't see it but I think I know what the problem is: she is resentful of her mother's devotion to me and it's a kind of sibling rivalry between us except that here, one of us is a dog!

Sometimes when she sees me on Jennifer's lap, she'll sidle over and try to unseat me! When I'm in a good mood, I'll give in to her and let her do it, but sometimes I can be mean, too, and I'll stay put and appeal to Jennifer for help with that pitiful, beguiling look she can't resist.

"Don't handle Eric so roughly," she'd chide Tanya. "He's so little he can break something if he falls!"

"I win," I'd smirk at a furious Tanya but that didn't help improve our relationship at all! But what did she expect? That she can step all over me and I'll take that sitting down?

The problem is we're about the same generation, in dog and child years so Tanya and I know exactly what is going on and we can't fool each other. She can see through my "sympathy" ruses and how Jennifer always falls for them and it gives me great satisfaction to see her grit her teeth and flounce away. Jennifer spoils her silly, and someone has to teach that missy that she can't always get what she wants—even if it has to be a dog that shows her that! It's for her own good to learn to be more responsible and less self-absorbed!

Jennifer spoils her silly and sometimes I worry what Tanya will become with all that spoiling; already, I can see the seeds of self-centeredness and willfulness flowering in her, suppressing the kindness and generosity of spirit that she told me one day was "uncool" for teens to show!

Some may ask who am I to talk like that when Jennifer spoils me, too, and I shamelessly lap it up. But, I'm different; no matter how I feel about myself, at the end of the day, I'm still a dog with a life span of fifteen years at most and I don't have to face any responsibilities in life or contribute anything to society. I will always have someone taking care of me and my only job is to be a pet and try to make my family happy, that's all.

But Tanya is a human. She has a life span of eighty or ninety years if all goes well. She will have responsibilities and is expected to contribute to society. She must look after herself eventually. So unlike me, she must learn to survive and even I can see that being so selfish and spoiled isn't a good start!

Jennifer sometimes wonders what I'm thinking of when I'm lying there watching them with half-closed eyes. Well, she might like to know that these are the kinds of thoughts that go through me, sometimes serious, sometimes frivolous and sometimes downright wicked but yes, dogs do reflect and worry for their families when they see that things aren't going the right way!

But then it's all wistful thinking because when you think of it, who will listen to the advice of the family dog?

CHAPTER | *Fourteen*

For days, the family had been discussing pet hotels, pet sitters and I wondered why. I heard my name mentioned several times but they always lowered their voices when I appeared and that bothered me a whole lot. I don't like it when people talk about me and I have no clue what it's all about. My experience with the end result of all the goings-on at the farm has left me nervous and jumpy whenever there's a buzz and I don't know what is happening.

Were they thinking of getting another dog? I decided grimly if they did that, I would spend every waking moment doing things to run the new dog out of the house.

"Jennifer knows very well I can't stand the sight and sound of any other dog within even one meter of me so if she does that to me, she deserves what will surely follow, just watch me!" I thought, incensed at what I saw as a betrayal of my loyalty and my love. Well, all right, I'm not the perfect dog but if they wanted to get another canine, they should at least ask me first what I thought!

In the end, I spent so much time thinking of what I would do to the new dog that I actually forgot to listen in to their conversations. I just presumed that it was all about getting another dog!

Then Jennifer started making calls and I heard her asking about pet boarding charges, cage or air conditioned single room and I realized with a shock that she was not bringing in a new dog but going to put ME somewhere.

I rushed over and pawed her urgently. Why? Why were they taking me away? I hadn't done anything recently that was anything new or worse than usual. Where were they taking me? I needed answers. What did they think, that dogs couldn't feel so nothing has to be explained to them?

Jennifer refused to be baited into any kind of conversation or explanation about my impending "trip" and what was worse, she wouldn't even meet my beseeching eyes. That wasn't a good sign because when Jennifer is guilty about something concerning me, it's never good news. But she did give me a hug and said, "Don't worry, Eric. Trust me; it'll only be for a few days."

That did reassure me a bit but a few days or an eternity, what difference did it make? I didn't want to go on any "trips" or spend even a single night away from my family. I would miss them terribly and besides, who in the world could take my idiosyncrasies? I became very down. My Mom asked me to trust her but why won't she look me in the eye? That could only be if she had something to hide!

It was a great blow to my ego that no matter how macho or indispensable I thought I was to the family, ultimately I was totally dependent on them, at their mercy and it was they, my owners and my masters who decide my fate, even whether I live or die or where I should go.

It was a demoralizing thought and I became so depressed I refused even my favorite snacks. Jennifer got real worried and after a couple of days she couldn't stand it anymore. She knew what was bothering me, of course and she took me out to the poolside so that Tanya could not listen in and smirk at my change of fortunes.

"Okay, Eric, let's talk," she said picking me up and putting

93

me on her lap on one of deck chairs around the pool. "Tanya and I are going for a trip to London next week and John will also be away on a business trip and we need someone reliable to look after you while we're all away. So we've been scouting around for the best place to put you but none of them seems good enough. So I've decided to put you at Aunt Meri's place where at least you won't be locked up in a cage and will have a home environment."

"Besides, it's safer there; you won't be exposed to all kinds of infections. You know, Molly, the Shih Tzu from downstairs suffered so much and nearly died from kennel cough she picked up at one of the so-called five-star pet hotels. I don't trust any of the pet hotels enough to put you there."

First I was relieved because my family still loved and wanted me, they were just trying to find someone to look after me because they had to go away for a while. But still I was horrified at the solution they had found for me and I nudged Jennifer in the ribs.

"Aunt Meri?" I whimpered. "Isn't she the one who threatened to microwave me?"

Jennifer saw the look of horror on my face and laughed, "You're thinking of the microwave oven thing again, aren't you? She was just kidding, actually she has a heart of gold, and it's just her mouth that gets carried away sometimes."

I shook my head violently, pawing at her arm and moving my body from side to side which Jennifer recognized as my objection to what she had just suggested.

No, no, not Aunt Meri!" I protested.

She stopped me gently in mid-shake and said, "Can you stop for a moment? You're making me dizzy with all that shaking!"

I stopped the onset of a tantrum immediately, I had to humor her now that my life was in her hands and throwing tantrums wasn't the best way to do that!

"But seriously," Jennifer continued. "All things considered, it'll be the best place for you. Aunt Meri has agreed to put her own dog, Scarlet, in her friend's place next door so you won't have to deal with another dog and before you know it, we'll be back!"

I'd just have to trust her because that's the way it is, no matter how much I object, in the end, I would still be bundled off to Aunt Meri's place, hoping for the best and praying for swift deliverance!

Tanya was surprisingly sweet, assuring me over and over again that everything would be all right and that she'd miss me. I was touched and that week, we put aside our recent differences and spats and became friends again. It was the best week for our relationship in a long time.

In a way, it was good that they warned me or rather that I forced a confession out of Jennifer of what was in store for me quite a few days before the event because as the days passed, I got used to the idea that I would be spending some time away from home.

When Jennifer laid the bags on the bed and started packing, I even found it exciting rather than upsetting. I pushed aside all of thoughts of my own not-so-exciting trip to hell and joined in the hustle and bustle of packing, pretending that I was going with them. I picked and fetched small items like socks and pulled out stockings and underwear from the luggage to play with when I thought Jennifer and Tanya weren't looking. But they were and I got an earful for messing up their packing. But I didn't mind because soon, when I was in hell, I thought, that "earful" would seem like music from heaven!

I didn't know exactly what day I was supposed to be "delivered" but I had become a little nervous in endless speculation, waking up each morning and wondering, is today the day? But we dogs are quite fatalistic in the way we manage and accept things beyond our control and if it seemed that it wasn't the day, I relaxed, let down my guard and got through the rest of the day quite happily.

Well, finally, the day I dreaded arrived. I knew because Jennifer got out what she called my "doggy bag," the big blue canvas sling bag with the picture of a big bone in front which she uses to put all my stuff inside, toys, water bottle, towel, snacks, when she took me to the beach or a picnic in the gardens. This time she put more things inside because I was going for a longer trip, adding even a few tins of dog food and my favorite soft toy, a much chewed and battered rabbit with both eyes and an ear missing.

I felt depressed watching my Mom prepare my "going away" bag because basically, I was very happy and comfortable in my own home and I didn't want my life disrupted, even for a week. I'd miss my Mom too much, all the silly little things I share with her and our midnight cuddles and the snacks under the quilt because if John knew about them, he would force us to listen to his long-winded lectures about overweight dogs with heart problems.

I put my front paws on Jennifer's knee and looked at her beseechingly.

Where were they going, why couldn't they take me with them?

Jennifer seemed to understand me and she said, "I wish I could take you along but we're going to London and you'll face quarantine on both sides for a total of seven months! Imagine being locked up in a cage for seven months! Isn't one week with Aunt Meri better by comparison?"

Locked up in a cage for seven whole months? No way! I had to agree finally that one week with Aunt Meri was indeed a better option and I resigned myself to it.

It was clear that the feeling of reluctance was mutual because I heard Jennifer talking to Aunt Meri on the phone and her voice was so loud that it actually wafted into the room from across the telephone lines.

"That dog is very troublesome you know," she was grumbling. "Well, he just has to obey the rules here and understand that no one here will hand feed him and under no circumstances is he allowed to sleep on anyone's bed! And I'm only taking in that nasty, dirty creature for you, remember that!"

Did she just call me a nasty, dirty creature? God, how I hated that woman's coarse and loud voice, it was hard to believe that she is the wife of a rich tycoon with everything money can buy; she is so downright abrupt, ungracious and loud-mouthed!

Her obvious reluctance to have me sent shivers down my spine and I thought of the witch, Cruella in the movie "One Hundred and One Dalmatians" that Tanya and I had watched one day on TV. That woman was real nasty and Aunt Meri reminded me of her and although Jennifer assured me over and over again that she wasn't all that bad, I wasn't convinced. But, if it was any comfort, at least I knew she wouldn't let any harm come to me because she would have to answer to Jennifer.

The day finally arrived and the whole family took me over to Aunt Meri's place. It was every dog's dream of a house, two floors of big, airy rooms that one could get lost in and a large garden filled with trees, flowers and soft springy grass. There were even small sparrows flitting from tree to tree, entertaining us with their chirpy little songs, and a couple of squirrels raced up the trees as we approached. It reminded me of my first home, the farm in Australia so much so that I almost expected my other Mom, Tracy, to run out of the shrubs to meet me as if there had never been five human years and over 3,000 miles of ocean between us!

97

Then Aunt Meri came out to greet us and a dark cloud descended on this paradise and the euphoria of the moment disappeared, as if destroyed by the dark spell of a witch. I shivered at the sight of her and hated myself for that. Where was the brash macho dog strutting around, manipulating everyone in the house?

"You'll be fine," Tanya whispered. "You know the saying that 'her bark is worse than her bite'? Well, that's Aunt Meri! She's actually much kinder than she wants to let on."

It was clear that Jennifer was upset to leave me. She lingered on, going over the instructions on my habits, my phobias, my heart medication, my vet, several times even when John reminded her they had to get to the airport on time.

I clung to her and refused to let go, screaming for all I was worth. Now that it was time for my family to go and leave me alone with these strange people in this strange place, I was frantic. What if something happened to Jennifer, John and Tanya and they never came back for me? Would I have to stay in this house with thousands of rules and regulations forever?

But you know, no matter how much of a fight we put up, dogs can never win, our human masters always overpower us by fair or foul means. Lisa, one of Aunt Meri's maids who is said to be very good with dogs came over and took me from Jennifer. I had to admit she did it with real ease, calmly unhooking my paws from Jennifer and physically remove me from my Mom, totally unfazed by my escalating screams and howls. She wisely brought me into the kitchen so that I couldn't see my family leave and kick up a bigger fuss.

Even from the kitchen, my sharp ears picked up the familiar sound of our car door slamming and I tried to struggle free to run after the car but Lisa held on tightly. She didn't smell like Jennifer at all, her body gave out a kind of earthy scent of human sweat mixed with talcum powder but it was not unpleasant. In fact, Lisa smelled of, you know, "mother" and I knew I could feel comfortable with her if I allowed myself to do so. But my body was stiff with determined rejection and later when I got closer to her, we had a good laugh over her comment that she felt she was carrying a piece of wood or dried meat that day!

She brought me to the kitchen window just in time to see my family's car going out of the gate and I started a fresh round of howling as I was reminded of the day I had been in a vehicle, standing up on my tiny hind legs to watch my whimpering mother, Tracy become a tiny dot and disappearing into the distance.

I stopped yelling when I realized that my family had gone and it wouldn't do me any good to get into Aunt Meri's bad books with all that din because until Jennifer and John came to get me, I was totally at her mercy.

I am, like any other dog, a pragmatic survivor and I knew that here I could not be my normal eccentric, short-tempered and bullying self. If there was a time I had to face my day of reckoning and learn a couple of lessons on how to live like a dog and not a boy, this was indeed the moment!

CHAPTER | *Fifteen*

The very first thing Aunt Meri did was to lay the down the rules to me. In her house, she said, dogs behaved like dogs and not royalty so no sleeping on beds, no peeing on carpets and getting away with it, no hand feeding, no excessive yelling, no talking unless spoken to, no begging for table scraps, no song and dance routines, no controlling of humans by manipulating them to go only to restaurants which allowed dogs, no, no, no, the list went on and on!

As I listened to the long list of disruptions to my daily routine and what I considered was my normal lifestyle, I didn't know how I was going to get through two weeks of Aunt Meri. Jennifer had said one week but later Lisa told me it was actually two weeks but Jennifer had lied to me to make the parting less painful if I thought it was only for a week. How could you lie to me, Mom? I was mad at Jennifer initially but later I had to admit that she was right, if I had known it was for as long as two weeks, I might have put up a fiercer resistance and traumatized everyone much more.

The first few days I was very lost, I didn't know where I was supposed to sleep or how I was supposed to eat and I realized that for all my show of strength, I was very dependent on my family doing things for me, even though I directed them on my preferences.

That night I was scared, real scared because the house was so big I literally disappeared in it. The whole family slept upstairs and they left a big dog basket outside the bedroom of Robert, Aunt Meri's son for me to sleep. But I didn't like it because it had the smell of another dog and probably Jennifer had forgotten to tell them that I am very finicky about personal hygiene, I don't sleep in baskets that had the body odor of another dog in it.

Jennifer had brought a few pieces of her clothing for me to sleep on and feel comfortable with her scent but nasty Aunt Meri refused to hear of such stuff and nonsense and put them away. I wished that day I was a boxer so that I could give her a real punch in the face, I was so mad at her for being that insensitive. That day, she really made me feel my seven kilos of empty, powerless fluff!

I have to be with people when I sleep and unlike our apartment where a light is always left on in case I needed to go to my toilet in the utility room behind the kitchen, Aunt Meri's household didn't believe in leaving any light on at night so the whole place was dark after everyone had gone to bed. The only light came from the street lamps outside and that was worse because the pale fingers of light streaming into the house created ghostly shadows on the walls which really spooked me up.

I knew I wasn't going to get a single minute of sleep unless I found some place other than that awful dog basket to bury myself in and shut out the spooky shadows on the walls. In the pale lamplight, I saw a small sofa with a collection of soft fat cushions just outside Aunt Meri's bedroom, the one she called her TV couch.

She had a thing about her sofas and had already made it clear that climbing onto them was a big no-no for me and this prohibition was non-negotiable. But I was so scared of the creepy shadows on the walls that I decided to break this most important rule of Aunt Meri's Code of Dog Regulations, jump onto the deep warm inviting TV sofa and hid my face inside the wonderfully soft, squeezy cushions. Blow Aunt Meri and her obsession with her sofas, I was sure I would be up and off that wretched piece of furniture at daybreak, before she woke up and no one would be any wiser!

But although the cushions hid the creepy shadows on the wall from me and I was physically quite comfortable, I lay awake thinking of my family for a long time. Where were they and were they thinking of me? Did Jennifer especially feel that same aching pain that I was feeling from missing her so much? The tears that had been gathering in my eyes the whole night spilled over and trickled slowly down my face. I could see my beloved Mom, Jennifer's face in front of me and her ridiculously childlike voice asking, "Do you think dogs can cry?"

"Yes, Mom, dogs do cry and in case you are enjoying yourself and not thinking of me, I wish you could see me crying now because I feel so alone and so far away from my family," I whispered as I sank at last into a fitful sleep.

My last thought was "Two weeks! How long exactly is two weeks?" Right now, it seemed like forever to me.

The minute I opened my eyes I knew I had overslept and been caught red-handed and I was right. Aunt Meri was standing over me, her arms ominously folded and before I could even move a muscle, she had caught hold of me and dumped me unceremoniously on the floor.

"Bad dog!" she shouted. "What did I tell you about not climbing up on the sofa? Don't let me catch you again!"

I glared at her but did not answer back as I would usually do with Jennifer, but I couldn't resist doing what I knew would irritate Aunt Meri—yawning nonchalantly right in her face—and to my deep satisfaction it did! This was the first of many run-ins I would have with "Cruella" as I called her in the days to come. In the end I solved my sleeping problem by bunking in with Lisa in the maid's room at night and although it didn't have an air conditioner, the powerful ceiling fan in the room made it tolerable for me.

I was hungry and I needed my morning snack but I didn't know where my snacks were and who was supposed to give them to me. Finally I decided that Lisa was the best bet and trotted downstairs to the kitchen to look for her. After all, anywhere was better than remaining upstairs with Aunt "Cruella."

A car sounded on the driveway and I dashed out to see whether it was Jennifer's car although I knew that it felt too soon to be two weeks but no one could blame me for hoping, I was pining for my family. Lisa saw me and said, "It's not your Mommy's car. Poor Eric, come with me because I have your snacks."

That settled my concerns about who was supposed to see to my food and when Lisa gave me my usual morning snacks, they had never tasted so good. By the end of that first day, I had studied everyone in that house and reached a decision about who to avoid and who to curry favor with.

Lisa was the sweetest and my greatest ally, Aunt Meri was to be avoided at all costs but Uncle Tom, her husband could be manipulated to side with me in any disputes with his wife. He saw me as this tiny helpless creature which needed protection and constantly chided Aunt Meri for being so rough with me and calling me names as if I didn't have any feelings.

He turned out to be a great guy, even if he appeared indifferent to everyone and everything around him. Aunt Meri complained endlessly about him, called him the mastermind of indifference and told everyone who would listen to her that even if there was an earthquake and the whole house tumbled down, Uncle Ton would continue sitting in front of the TV flicking channels till the TV too collapsed at his feet!

Well, Aunt Meri was right about me in some ways because I could be really mean when I got mad and one of the things I wanted to do was get her into trouble as many times as possible and it wasn't long before I found a way of doing that.

Whenever she walked past me and I saw that Uncle Tom was around, I would put on my best act of cringing and running to a corner whimpering pitifully. Uncle Tom would immediately jump to my defense and demand to know what Aunt Meri had done to me.

"I never even touched that sly devious animal," she protested, matching my triumphant grin with a glare. "Can't you see the way he's grinning? Obviously trying to do me in. I never saw a creature so cunning!"

"Animal indeed! I do have a name, you know, woman!" I muttered under my breath as I slipped away, leaving them to argue over me.

Later I heard Aunt Meri complain to someone on the phone about my evil ways of getting her into trouble with Uncle Tom but I could see that she wasn't seriously angry, in fact she sounded almost proud that the dog she was taking care of was smart enough to think of such tricks to "discredit" and outsmart her. It almost seemed that she was boasting about me! I was amazed! Did she actually respect me for being able to do her in?

I shook my head, somewhat bemused. Who could understand these mad, totally incomprehensible and unpredictable humans? Just beats me!

After that, I fancied she looked at me with new respect and didn't dare put me down so much and things became a little better between us. Dogs are adaptable because they don't have a choice. Adapt to survive; and wait. We spend a lot of time waiting—for someone to feed us, to take us out for walks, to play with us, to groom us and the hardest and most painful of all is waiting for our masters to return for us. And always there is this worry: what if something happens to them and they never come back? How will I live without them?

I think I never really slept the whole of those two weeks; I always had one ear in full navigation just in case the family returned to get me and I wasn't ready. Every time a car came into the driveway or someone came to the door, I would be streaking out to see if it was Jennifer, John or Tanya. I missed them so much my body actually felt physically heavy with that burden.

I knew they called at least every other day to find out how I was because I could hear Aunt Meri saying, "Don't worry, he's fine. He's a tough cookie, that one!"

I was always hanging around the phone waiting for news of my family and when they called, my heart would be bursting with joy because it meant they were alive and well and they were thinking of me and I knew they would be back for me. A couple of times I could tell they asked her to put me on the phone but there was not a chance of that happening with Aunt Meri, it wasn't that she was cruel or anything like that, she simply didn't believe in carrying the dog-man relationship that far, to what she called "disgusting smooching on the phone!"

But one day, an amazing thing happened, Aunt Meri was out when the phone rang and Lisa answered it. She saw me hanging around as usual and she called me over.

"Eric, it's your mommy! You want to talk to her?"

Boy, did I indeed!

I needed no second invitation to talk to Jennifer or even John or Tanya. Lisa held the phone next to my ears and the voice of my beloved Mom, Jennifer, floated across thousands of miles to reach me, telling me to hang in there because it was only one more week to going home. I felt as if I had died and gone to heaven.

I pawed violently at the receiver upsetting the phone from its stand because I wanted to see and hug her, I wanted to cover her face with a million lashings of my tongue, but thousands of miles separated us and all I had was that instrument called a phone which miraculously conveyed her voice to me.

I whimpered and barked my responses telling her how much I missed her and John and Tanya. Could she really hear me?

"Come and get me soon, Mommy!" I screamed as Lisa removed the phone from my ear.

It's amazing how we are all creatures of necessity and how quickly we can adapt to changed circumstances for survival. The first day I refused to eat the food Lisa had been told to leave on my dog bowl in the kitchen. I wanted to be hand-fed as usual. I think the soft-hearted Lisa would have given in and hand-fed me if Aunt Meri hadn't insisted that rules were rules and I had to eat by myself.

"Just leave the food there and if he gets really hungry, he will eat," she said and although I hate to admit it, she was right.

I held out for two meals, surviving on the three snacks a day Lisa was allowed to give me although she did sneak in an extra piece for me. But for an active, slightly overweight dog like me, that wasn't enough and I got real hungry and agitated as I watched Aunt Meri calmly take the dog bowl of untouched food away and empty it into the trash can that she had "dog proofed" by putting a heavy marble slab on the lid. There was no way in hell she was going to let a dog reduce her to hanging up plastic bags for trash as my Mom did!

The hungry rumblings in my tummy were growing louder and I was ready to cave in and eat by myself but pride held me back, I didn't want Aunt Meri to win this war with me. This went on for two days but by the third day, I was so hungry that I could not fight any more.

Let Aunt Meri have her "I knew I would win" look, I was too hungry to care. As soon as she put the food bowl down, I walloped everything and disappeared into the kitchen to lick my wounds of defeat but in extenuating circumstances, I guess even a dog had to be practical. Lisa, bless her soul, called me a good boy and rewarded me with a piece of dog food against Aunt Meri's instructions so at least I felt I had gainsaid her in some way.

During the day, I spent most of my time downstairs in the garden chasing butterflies and birds and challenging the cat from the house next door or following Lisa around as she did her chores. But it was just passing time. There was no soul or heart in anything I did and I definitely didn't want to do anything that would mark the house as my territory because it wasn't.

I didn't want to do the song and dance thing. If there were visitors, I would take a peek and if they weren't my family, I would just disappear into the kitchen without even a courtesy bark. It wasn't my territory and I had no obligation to protect anyone in this house, nor any right to stop anyone from coming to visit.

Aunt Meri took full credit for what she boasted to everyone was "the taming of a shrew dog" but when she triumphantly informed Jennifer of the change in me, no more song and dance nonsense, eating by myself, no picking of fights with anyone, human or dog, my Mom told me later she got real worried. You see, Jennifer knows that I can be quiet and obedient only if I am ill or drop dead depressed.

Once, when I was about one year old, John got so exasperated by my increasing willfulness that he decided to send me to an obedience school and it was an experience that he, Jennifer, me and the trainer didn't forget for a long time.

At one year old, rearing to go at life and feeling on top of the world, I was arrogant, aware of my perfect breeding and style, overly confident and totally out of control. So John thought that a stint at an established obedience school with a very high success rate of taming "unmanageable" dogs would instill some good values in me.

I had heard that obedience school was where they whipped you into subservience; I mean, the very word obedience reeked of military style discipline and was enough to make any dog shiver!

I told John and Jennifer I didn't want to go, I didn't need obedience training because I would turn over a new leaf on my own and be good but my word was not good enough for them. I had broken it so many times that it wasn't worth the bark it was delivered in any more!

So I was bundled into the car, kicking and spitting and driven out to the suburbs where the training school was. I was furious, because as usual, no one would listen to me and they just decided arbitrarily what was good for me and as we approached the school, I made up my mind that I would get myself expelled.

As I expected, the school was like a military camp surrounded by a sturdy fence and the only entrance was a huge, ugly wrought iron gate with the largest padlocks I had ever seen. I shuddered at this prison-like facility and realized I would need all my wits and destructive skills to get myself thrown out of it. After the usual registration and checking in, they didn't allow John and Jennifer to go in with me, but instead, they could watch me from a glass panel outside.

"My name is Kevin and I'm going to be your trainer today, Eric," the guy who took me said.

I hated him immediately and decided to give him a hard time so that they would expel me as soon as possible.

"God, what a ninny he is," I thought giving Kevin my best stare and snarl performance.

The place was crawling with dogs, most like me with behavioral problems so it was a noisy, snarling, barking and growling crowd. After an initial surveillance, I decided that the best way to create problems was to incite a revolt of some sort; the group of canines milling restlessly around looked ready for any excuse to pick a fight so it would be easy. I grinned, thinking of what a dog uprising could do to this detention center for dogs and my devious thoughts must have shown on my face because I saw Kevin looking at me worriedly.

"Potential trouble, that one," I heard him saying to his colleague. "Most Pomeranians are, so better keep a look out for him."

It was annoying, the way he was defaming my breed, and I decided that, all the more, since it was trouble he was expecting from a Pomeranian, I couldn't possibly disappoint him!

I waited till the trainers had got the dogs into some kind of order before escaping from Kevin and running into the rows of disgruntled canines, taking care to stay within the smaller ones so that I would not be trampled upon by the bigger and more aggressive dogs when things got rough.

My song and dance number, always a hit in the agitation department, incited a riot of catastrophic proportions as the dogs, already chaffing from the control they were unaccustomed to, leaped into action and merged into a mass of flying fur, bared fangs and deafening howls.

The trainers had a terrible time thundering out orders and trying to separate the dogs before they got hurt while Kevin caught hold of me and gave me such a tongue lashing, that my ears burned for hours after that. He could really swear and it was a blessing that my family couldn't hear what I thoroughly deserved from the other side of the glass panel.

It took a good half-hour to restore order and get the dogs seated again and the trainers were furious with me. They isolated me and put me in a corner by myself with Kevin watching over me but that suited me fine because I hated being with the other fidgety, drooling dogs anyway. What didn't agree with me was the fact that I hadn't been expelled yet, despite staging an uprising of all the dogs. So I decided it was time to enact Plan B.

The gate to the field in which we were doing our exercises was ajar and that put a very wicked idea into my head. I waited till the "sit, stand, and down" routine was in progress before streaking back to the other dogs barking out insults at them, "fat, ugly" "wrinkled, smelly" "balding, slack jaw" —I spat out everything I could think of and, as expected, it inflamed the thirty-odd dogs, mostly spoiled pedigrees with impeccable papers. They threw "sit, stand and down" to the wind and traded insults with me. One overweight, drooling and really ugly bulldog type even resorted to profanities and my, could he swear almost as well as Kevin! Just showed what kind of family he came from and I told him that much!

When things got really heated up, I dashed to the gate, pushed it wide open and ran out of the training area with all thirty screaming, howling dogs hot on my tail. This was getting dangerous because if they managed to reach me, I could be trampled flat in this stampede of dogs three times bigger than me or bitten to a pulp especially by the outraged bulldog I had called "wrinkly, balding and slack-jawed." In this mood of aggression I had incited, no one would spare me and it was not in my Plan B to get killed or seriously mauled.

Fortunately, I found a writing table with a space underneath that I figured I could just manage to crawl under if I flattened myself as I had seen the farm cats do. I had just finished crawling inside when I felt my tail which was still sticking out being pulled really hard. One of the dogs had gotten to me and was trying to rip my tail off! I wasn't about to become the first tail-less Pomeranian in the world so I tugged hard and with a yelp of pain, managed to free my tail just as scores of panting noses arrived to tear me apart.

The trainers, with Jennifer in tow, had also arrived and, a lot of shouting and protesting dogs later, order was restored once again with all the dogs, except me, being led back to the training area.

I heard Jennifer calling me, "It's all right, and you can come out now."

I hesitated knowing that after what I had done, I would surely face my judgment day and even Jennifer could not possibly let this go, unpunished. So I stayed resolutely inside till I had extracted a promise from her not to overdo the punishment thing. I was really scared because I thought maybe I had overstepped my limits this time especially if any of the other dogs had been hurt by the stampede. My family could be presented with a long and hefty vet bill and I was real worried now. Why hadn't I thought of this before I started my rampage?

I finally crawled out in surrender mode and Jennifer immediately broke her promise and for the first time in my life so far, I got a spanking from her with dire promises of more when we reached home.

Kevin came over to tell my parents that the center couldn't take me because I was too disruptive and had caused some damage which they would have to pay.

Jennifer and even John nagged me all the way home, warning me not make a squeak till they gave me permission to do so. When we reached home, they banished me to the kitchen to do what John called some "soul searching and reflection" to atone for my wicked ways.

If there's one thing I hate, it's being ignored by my family and Jennifer knew that being sent to Coventry was a far greater punishment than all the ranting and even spanking and she was right. I was so depressed I fell asleep on the cold kitchen floor without daring to ask for any food. It's just me; when I'm really depressed, I crawl into some place and sleep it off.

So that was it. My obedience training ended even before it started! And what was even better, Jennifer and John never dared mention the subject again!

CHAPTER Sixteen

The day started drizzly and gray but nothing could dampen my spirits because the night before, Lisa had told me that today was the day Jennifer and John were coming to get me. She looked kind of sad though, because I think she got used to me running around, minding everyone's business and giving the cats hell. She told me that I was far more interesting than Scarlet who was too obedient to be, you know, fun and even Aunt Meri grudgingly admitted that it was entertaining to watch me get into all kinds of scraps. I think that she would rather die than admit it but in her own way, she would miss me, too.

Well, to be honest, I knew I would never forget Lisa, too, and all our little conspiracies to cover up my crimes from Aunt Meri's sharp eyes. One day she even took the blame for something I did and I was very touched. I mean, as far as I know, the dog is usually blamed for everything and I'm used to defending myself from false accusations but I've never had a human prepared to take the blame for what I did!

And when she saw Aunt Meri's precious rose shrubs dug up, she would quickly put them back together before I was found out.

We shared some other really bizarre secrets as well. One day, when she was dusting around the area, Lisa took down a small metal pot from the family altar in the dining room and showed me the ashes inside.

"Look, Eric," she whispered. "These are the ashes of Aunt

Meri's father-in-law! Imagine a dead man is inside here!"

For a dog who is supposed to be aging five times faster than a human, it's understandable that I am terrified of death so it really spooked me up to hear this. I jumped up to get away from the pot and the sudden movement swept it from Lisa's hands.

Both of us froze as we watched the ashes flying out of the pot and Lisa's flailing hands instinctively trying to catch it. She looked so ridiculous trying to catch the ashes that I had this sudden impulse to laugh but I suppressed it out of respect for her deep distress. Besides, it was all my fault that Lisa was now in this fix.

Horror of horrors! We both knew that Aunt Meri would have a fit if she knew what had just happened so Lisa quickly took a small brush and swept what ashes could be salvaged into the pot, adding a little more from the small charcoal stove she quickly started up, to fill the pot to its original level.

It would be our little secret that Aunt Meri's father-in-law now shared his pot with quite a bit of charcoal ashes and Lisa, much to my amusement, cautioned me not to let slip. God, did she forget I am a dog and speaks a language no one understands? And besides, I grew very fond of Lisa so I would never split on her. Her secret would be very safe with me indeed!

But from that day on, I steered clear of the family altar because it gave me the creeps to think of what I likened as "a genie in the bottle" staring right at me. I heard my Mom arguing with someone before that dogs can see the spirits of dead people. I don't know whether that is true or not because I haven't actually seen any but I have felt their presence.

Once my Mom took me for a drive and on the way home, she took a short-cut through an old graveyard and it was pitch dark. No one told me it was a graveyard but I started feeling uneasy as soon as she turned into that road and the fur that always stood up in a line along my backbone when I am frightened started standing up for all it was worth.

"Hey, Mom, turn back, let's get out of this place, it's really spooking me up!" I whimpered but she couldn't turn back without driving into the graveyard to make a U-turn, which would be even worse. So we went right on but I could see by the way she was looking straight ahead that she was regretting taking that road, too.

Then I felt it—a kind of dark presence looking in at us from the right side of the car window and I screamed, flinging myself at the shadow pasted there trying to drive it away but my body only touched the cold glass of the window and the shadow remained there staring at us till the car emerged from that dark graveyard road into the welcoming glare of the main road again. My fur was all on end and I was foaming at the mouth from the intensity of my "attack" on the dark shadow. I don't know who looked more ghastly, the spirit or me!

I had a second brush with the supernatural not long after. On the fourth floor of our condo block was a Japanese family who had a small boy named Masao, about four years old. He was the cutest, most sweet-natured child I ever saw and somehow I liked him well enough to allow him to touch me and play with me, within limits, which was unusual because I normally hate children.

We often met in the elevator when Jennifer brought me out and his mother took him for a swim or just to play downstairs. Masao would walk alongside us and I even allowed it when Jennifer let him hold me once but just for a while because she was afraid I would turn nasty and snap at him.

One day something terrible happened. Masao fell from his fourth floor bedroom, broke his skull and died instantly. No one could believe it. That morning, we met on the elevator and he had just learned to say the word "Pomeranian" or "Pom chan" in Japanese and was repeating it over and over again, making everyone laugh. And now he was, what? Dead? Silenced forever?

Impossible! Impossible! I ran around in circles denying it. But it was true. Masao was dead and a sadness descended on the whole block of residents including me because the chubby cheerful little boy had been so much a part of our lives and made everyone laugh with his toothless smiles and winsome attempts at speaking English was dead. He was the only child I had been able to relate to without losing my cool and when they went to see him at the funeral parlor, I couldn't go of course because dogs weren't allowed. So I would never see him again or so I thought!

Masao's death affected me more than I cared to admit. Why did I spend so much time replaying that death scene over and over in my mind? There it was again—that chilling and sobering moment when I stuck out my head, looked up, and saw little Masao leaning from that fourth floor window.

That was the moment when I just froze and couldn't do a thing to save him!

"Stop, Masao, stop! Get back in!" I tried to scream but nothing came out of my usually cooperative voice chords. I couldn't believe that for the first time in my life, when I really needed it, the most powerful organ in my body had failed me!

Tanya had once taken a bet for real money with her friends that the vibrations from my roars could make papers fly and together we had won that bet, bottoms up!

A couple walked by, laughing happily at some stupid joke totally unaware of the suspense and tragedy that was unfolding four floors above them.

"Stop your chattering and do something," I panted but they couldn't hear me and walked right on by.

There was a gleeful gurgle as Masao swung his tiny body over the edge of the window, a gurgle that quickly changed to shrieks of terror as he lost his balance and hurled right past me to land with a thud on the stone pavement below.

I watched, fascinated, as that little broken body twitched several times and rivulets of crimson blood started to flowed everywhere like the bony fingers of a witch.

It was at that moment I found my voice at last and, like an unstoppable machine gun, I bellowed out belated distress calls, over and over again. They brought out several neighbors and the crescendo of shrieks that followed broke the late afternoon tranquility with blood-chilling precision.

I didn't know how long I went on what I admitted later was in fact not only about Masao but also about the humbling realization that I was, after all, just this huge big mind and ego trapped in a tiny dog body with very serious limitations. I didn't stop even when I felt my whole body growing limp from lack of air and I realized too late, that I was going to pass out.

"No," I protested. "Not me, passing out like that simpering poodle, Mimi, and her fainting spells? Over my dead body!"

But there was no fighting with the powers that be and the last I saw was Jennifer's white anxious face peering at me before I fell into that humiliating pit of shame.

When I came to, the first thing I saw was steel mesh wire and all hell broke loose inside me. There is something I can never ever stand or accept and that is being locked up in a cage, the indignity of such restraint just kills me! Who had done that to me? A rage was building up in me, so great that I hardly felt any pain as I threw my body repeatedly against the wire netting that kept me caged up at what looked like Dr. Harris, the vet's place.

"Let me out of here! Let me out!" I yelled, never stopping my assault, not even when I felt my skin break into multiple cuts and drew blood. The commotion created a panic among the other dogs and started a revolt against steel wires and vets.

"Come on, louder, louder," I incited everyone. "Together we can do this!"

One of the vet's assistants, a thick-set, ugly girl called Mina burst into the room and tried to intimidate us into subservience with a cane she brought angrily down on a stainless steel table top with the abusive force of a prison warden.

"What an utter bitch!" I screamed. "Fancy treating sick animals like that!"

I have a score to settle with that one because once when no one was looking, she brought that cane down on me, with just enough pressure not to cause any visible injuries but to give me some painful moments. Of course I ran to Jennifer to complain, complete with tail in between my legs and pitiful, accusing eyes fixed on my tormentor but I couldn't prove a thing simply because I couldn't make myself understood verbally and Mina got away with it, smirk glint in her eyes and all. And I vowed I would get even with her someday.

Mina continued cracking her cane on the stainless steel table and running it viciously against the cages of her rebellious charges till the last barking had died down to scared submissive whimpers.

All except mine.

"You witch!" I screamed. "You should be a butcher not a vet's assistant and I'm going to get you fired if that's the last thing I do!"

I doubled my verbal assault so ferociously that even Mina backed off my cage but I wasn't going to let her get away with it this time. At the risk of losing my voice for the next few days, I kept up my assault till Dr. Stephen, the night vet, came in to check out the commotion. By then I had figured out that if I stuck my paw out of a tear in the mesh wire, I could widen the hole and get the catch of the lock to spring up.

As the door of the cage swung open, I controlled my instinctive desire to savage Mina because this was my chance to get even with her. Putting on my best "poor victimized helpless creature" act, I lowered my voice to the soft pitiful whimpers that never failed to tug at heart strings and crawled out of my cage, slowly, painfully making sure that the cuts on my body from my own violent assault on the restraining mesh wire were visible to Dr. Stephen.

Dragging my "battered" body across the cold, hard-tiled floor, trembling and terrified, I crawled past the gap-mouthed Mina—still with the incriminating cane in her hand—toward Dr. Stephen, whimpering as if my life depended on it. I could feel the warm trickle of blood running cooperatively down my left leg and I knew I had nailed Mina as the night vet turned to her and thundered, "How could you hit one of our charges? How do you expect us to explain to his owners why he is injured when he was brought in without any cuts or injuries? Do you want us to be sued?"

"But, Dr. Stephen, I swear I never laid a hand on him, he injured himself," Mina started to protest.

"How? He took a knife and cut himself?" Dr. Stephen cut her short with the fury of a vet who really did not need such trouble on his shift. "You're fired and be thankful that we can cover up this incident by telling his owner he injured himself by throwing himself against the cage."

"But that's what really happened!" Mina tried to protest.

"How do you know? Did you see it? Did I see it? What does it look like—a limping dog and you, with a cane in your hand?"

I couldn't believe it! What poetic justice! My score with Mina was settled that day and when the night vet was not looking, I did a little jig. Never again would I have to suffer Mina's smelly armpits as she deliberately tucked me under her arm every visit to the vet. I had to suffer the lingering stench on my body and fur for days afterwards till I learned to topple and spill Jennifer's cologne onto the floor and roll myself in it.

In the morning, Jennifer picked me up and I endured her "fuss and pamper till death do us part" kisses and hugs for ten minutes before pushing her away. Didn't she know that any pressure on my body caused me pain? But I held my tongue stoically like a man because I had done enough whimpering for all the wrong reasons the last few days to last me a lifetime! And now, when I should be whimpering for the acceptable reason of real pain, I had to shut up and keep a stiff upper lip!

"*Ce le vie*!" I thought dourly. "Such is life, even for a dog!"

It was only later in the night that I sobered up as the events of the last few days started to invade my mind again. But I didn't feel so guilty any more for not being able to save Masao because I felt I had paid for that failure by my collapse and the pain from my injuries.

But was it enough? After he died, I was so glad I had been able to make him happy. Masao was a little boy you just didn't feel like doing a single nasty thing to.

But a few days after his death, strange things began to happen to me. I starting dreaming about Masao and the dreams and illusions were so real that I actually saw him standing in front of me, smiling and waving as he always did and asking me to go with him because he was lonely where he was now and he missed me.

These dreams were disturbing but of course there was no way I could tell Jennifer about them and ask her for advice. This was one of the times that I really felt the lack of communication between dog and his master simply because there is no common language. How I wish the Japanese would hurry up and invent something which would allow a dog to talk to his master!

Things came to a head one night seven days after the accident. The family had just finished dinner when I felt a presence all over me, trying to take possession of me. I screamed but nothing came out as I fell onto the floor, eyes turning and the breath choking out of me as if someone was squeezing my neck. From a very long distance I heard the scuffle of Jennifer and John picking me up and their frightened voices calling the vet's emergency number.

I knew with deep clarity that it was Masao coming to take me to be his playmate—that was what the dreams had been about, Masao telling me he was coming for me. No, I cried, I don't want to go yet, I haven't finished with life! I started talking to the little boy, pleading with him not to take me. I knew Masao would listen because he had been a sweet and kind boy who would never hurt anyone consciously and I was right.

Even as I pleaded for my life, I felt the heavy presence suddenly lift and the choking sensation in my throat eased immediately. My breathing became normal again and I was able to struggle free of Jennifer's arms.

Masao had heard my pleas and given me back my life! I had a glimpse of his sad face as it slowly retreated and faded into the distance. I never dreamed about him again.

So, yes, I guess you can say that dogs do feel and see spirits!

But Masao and spirits were far from my very much alive mind that day when I was finally going home. I was so excited to see my family again I just couldn't sit still the whole morning, straining my ears for the familiar sound of a car entering the driveway. It had to happen, of course, just at the exact moment I was at the back of the house answering the call of nature but my razor-sharp ears had picked up and recognized Jennifer's car and her way of driving and I ran, helter skelter, drops of my unfinished business following me all the way! I would regret that later when the fur around my legs started to stink of urine but for now, nothing else mattered.

It had been a long and educational two weeks during which time I had learned to eat by myself and sleep in the maid's room without a night lamp or air conditioning and no one took me out anywhere so I had to entertain myself by roaming around the gardens terrorizing the birds and neighborhood cats and stealing my own snacks. But it proved that I could do it and Aunt Meri was right when she said, "just give him a couple of days with me and he'll be a changed dog."

But it was also true how quickly I could "unchange" myself when I returned to my own home and my real life of hand-feeding, sleeping on a bed in an air conditioned room, making sure my family does not go anywhere without me. After two weeks with Aunt Meri, I was ready to be spoiled silly again and this time I felt, I really deserved it!

I hoped Aunt Meri wouldn't influence Jennifer to carry on the good work she felt she had done disciplining me but even if she tried, she wouldn't succeed because I know how to twist Jennifer round my little paw and she could never resist me. In the end, I needn't have worried because my family felt so guilty about dumping me with Aunt Meri, they upped the spoiling and pampering at least a couple of notches and my God, was that one hell of a homecoming indeed!

The first thing I did after the effusive greetings and hundreds of tongue lashings I dispensed generously to my family, was to complain about Aunt Meri to Jennifer right in her face, wicked ungrateful dog that I was!

Whining and pawing, I directed Jennifer to my complaints with surreptitious looks at Aunt Meri, which made them all laugh. They knew exactly what I was up to!

Aunt Meri surprised me by coming over and giving me a

122

playful cuff in the ears.

"Just look at him trying to tell tales on me," she said good naturedly. "I want to put on record I never touched or bullied him except when he broke the house rules and then he had to be disciplined but even then, it was just a couple of light spanks."

I looked at her with new respect and decided Aunt Meri wasn't such a bad sort after all. I made a mental note not to give her such a hard time when next she came to visit us.

My first trip away from home and, apart from a few teething problems and light skirmishes with Aunt Meri, it hadn't been all that bad after all! Most important, I had proven to myself that I could survive under extenuating circumstances!

CHAPTER | Seventeen

I *can't believe it.* Today's my birthday and I'm eight dog years old! I hardly dare to calculate how old I am in human years because I think I would be middle aged! The amazing thing is I don't feel any major changes at all in the way I think and behave as five or six years ago and my energy levels certainly haven't dropped very much either. If anything, I seem more active than before.

My family wanted to throw a small party for me because eight was a good number but as Tanya pointed out logically, who would we invite? I was so hostile toward other dogs that the party would surely end up with fights, growls, snarls and threats instead of festivities and good cheer! Besides, I was more likely to threaten and drive away my guests, both canine and human, than welcome them! So we finally settled for peace and a family dinner at home, complete with my favorite chicken breast meat and ice cream cake.

How the years have flown and it doesn't seem so long ago that I was this tiny fluffy puppy standing up on my wobbly legs to wave goodbye to my Mom, Tracy, as the pet transport van carried me further and further away from all that I knew and loved to an uncertain future.

But except for a few bumps along the way, life has been very good to me. I really have nothing to complain about except that it frightens me that the days, months and years are passing so fast. Jennifer says that with good veterinary care these days, dogs do live up to more than fifteen years but do I want to live that long and see myself at the human age of 105? I need to think about it especially when I think of Pop and imagine myself becoming like that!

Once I went for a walk with Jennifer and we met a dog from the neighborhood, a Golden Retriever called Pop, who was so old that he walked like a snail on unsteady legs and his fur had dropped out, leaving patches of bare wrinkled skin. Even his eyes and face were slack and drooping and yet he must once have been an active, beautiful dog, just like me now.

I shuddered to think that someday I would be like him, trapped in a disintegrating aged body of aches and pains, not wanting to live but afraid to die and leave my family. Lately, I've become so afraid of growing old and ugly that everyday I am looking at myself in the mirror, just to make sure eyes, nose, mouth, fur, all are still intact!

I'm very proud of my fine Pomeranian features, my broad chest and my glorious plume of a tail, as Tanya always accuses me and I admit it, I'm woefully vain! Whenever I come back from the groomers and Danny has gone a bit overboard with the shearers and shorn my beautiful coat almost to the quick and I see my tail, hairless and curled up like a pig's tail, it breaks my heart and I feel very small and ugly. I keep a low profile and can't wait for my fur to grow and fill out a bit so that I look more presentable. I guess we dogs are in some ways a lot like humans: when we look good, we feel good! It's a thing called self-confidence!

When I go out and people tell Jennifer stuff like what a beautiful dog she's got, my heart swells with pride and although I pretend to look nonchalant and "hell devil may care," deep inside I am extremely happy and reassured of my good looks. A couple of days ago, we watched with great interest, a TV program on pets and the show host, bless his soul, said that small dogs age slower and live longer. They brought to the show several toy breeds, a silky terrier and a Pomeranian, said to be twelve years old but still looking and acting so young and beautiful.

I was so proud to be a Pomeranian and I pawed Jennifer excitedly, leaving scratches on her arm but she didn't take it to heart because she knew I was trying to tell her that I wanted to grow old looking that young!

Jennifer knows how fussy I am about my personal hygiene and in that sense I am more like a cat than a dog. Every morning, the minute I wake up, I start the day with a meticulous grooming regime, washing my face with my paws, exactly like a cat, making sure my eyes especially are cleaned of every single trace of discharge and my paws are licked clean of every speck of dust. Every time I relieve myself in my "toilet" I will rush straight out to Jennifer or whoever is in the house and demand that the soiled newspaper be changed immediately. I have to have fresh newspapers every time and if it's not done; you can expect me to relieve myself in the bathmat in the toilet to protest this "neglect."

Jennifer thinks I must have been a cat in my previous life but the truth is that I was born on a farm and for the first most important weeks of my life, I lived alongside the farm cats and kittens and couldn't tell the difference between cats and dogs. So when I saw them washing and preening themselves, I started following them and it soon became a habit. My Mom, Tracy, being a semi-retired show dog herself, encouraged and cultivated in us this habit of personal pride and I never lost sight of that.

How many times have I wished that I could tell Jennifer about this and all the other things in the first two months of my life which greatly shaped the way I am so that she could understand me and some of my oddities a lot better! But it's almost impossible to communicate effectively to her some of the deeper things I say, do and think. Unfortunately we don't share any common language so there will always be a lot of empty spaces in our relationship but we make the best of it and after sometime, these empty spaces don't seem to matter that much.

One day I woke up with a terrible pain in my left hind leg and it took a while before I remembered jumping down from a chair the previous night after using it to get at a packet of snacks. The family had gone out without me because they had to attend a function in a place where dogs weren't allowed, and I was a little mad even though I knew I should understand. But I'm not a very patient or tolerant dog —a character flaw of Pomeranians, I am often reminded—so I was resentful that I was left at home on a Saturday night with to do than wait for them to return. So I decided to entertain myself by figuring out ways to reach a shelf where I knew Jennifer kept some of my snacks.

The shelf wasn't very high up and I reckoned that if I climbed onto a low chair I could just manage to drag a packet of snacks down. But I couldn't reach the tantalizing, neatly stacked bags which stayed stubbornly just out of reach and in a huff I leaped down from the chair without taking the usual precaution of jumping lightly and landed heavily on my legs.

I felt a twinge of pain in my left hind leg but most of it went off after some time so I resolutely ignored the slight lingering ache and parked myself at the front door to wait for the family to return. They came back quite late and made a fuss of me because they felt bad about leaving me behind. I seized the opportunity to make them take me out for a drive because I was bored to the hilt with being cooped up in the apartment the entire afternoon and night.

A drive to one of our regular coffee shops for a late night supper later, I forgave them and on the way back, I felt the slight pull in my hind leg again but it didn't bother me very much so I let it be. A squeak from me and I knew Jennifer would rush me to the vet and I certainly wasn't prepared to spend the night in that place, locked up in a cage while they "observed" me!

But by the morning, the pain was so bad that I couldn't hide it from Jennifer because I was virtually hobbling on three legs and dragging the fourth. Of course, she bundled me into the car and took me to the vet immediately.

"Just a sprained ankle, nothing more! I don't need to go to the vet," I protested feebly but Jennifer wouldn't hear of it. As usual her driving was hair-raising when she was stressed up and anxious and I was near throwing up by the time we reached the vet. I didn't know which was worse; the pain in my leg or my Mom's driving!

The minute Dr. Takagi, the new vet, looked at my leg and the X-rays, I knew I'd had it.

"Not a simple sprain or anything like that," he said, re-affirming my fears. "Eric has a very badly displaced knee cap probably from jumping and he needs an operation to push it back and a metal plate to hold it in place."

My face paled underneath all that fur. The long list of things Dr. Takagi planned to do to me didn't sound at all pleasant and I looked around instinctively for an escape route. But there was none and anyway, who was I kidding? The pain had to be fixed sooner or later.

Jennifer was distraught so she said the first thing that came into her head: "Eric, how many times have I told you not to jump? The trouble with these Pomeranians is that they think they are five times bigger than they are!"

I smiled apologetically at her but inside I was seething. Ouch, that really hurt and anyway, what was the point of bringing all these up now, woman? I was the one in pain after all and I was the one having to go through all those operations and metal pins. What about a bit of sympathy, here? I could really use some, I growled angrily.

Okay, okay, I know I shouldn't have jumped from such a great height on my little Pomeranian legs but sometimes, you know, it's so sickening to be locked up in this tiny body and be able to do so little physically when your heart and spirits are as big as that of a Saint Bernard! Yes, there're times when I am so sick of being a little toy breed, I want to jump, and leap and fly like the big boys! I fear the tiny heart beating in my chest will get so big it will just leap out!

What kind of demented thoughts were going through me? Must be the tranquillizer Dr. Takagi had just injected which was making me light-headed.

I don't know at which point I was knocked out but the next time I regained consciousness, I was in a cage and the room was filled with chrome and stainless steel. My tongue felt like it was too big for my mouth and I needed water badly but when I tried to get up, I realized that my left hind leg was in a hard cast and I couldn't bend it.

I remembered what Dr. Takagi had said about an operation and metal pins in my knee cap. Good Lord, they had gone and done that to me and now I would have more pieces of metal in my body for the rest of my life! For a moment I panicked at the thought of these foreign matters in my body. What if the metal became old and rusty, or what if the pins gave way inside? I started to imagine stray metal pins floating all over my body, puncturing my organs, one by one!

The place was deadly quiet except for the very soft murmur of the air conditioning and I panicked again, for real this time. Where was everyone? Had they handicapped me, put all kinds of metals in my body, locked me in this cage and were now leaving me to die? Even as these thoughts flashed through my mind, I chided myself. Really, how could I think such things? Jennifer would never do that to me but still, there was this disturbing thought, "Where IS everyone?"

As if my thoughts had leaked out and penetrated the outside world at last, the frosted glass door squeaked open and a green-gowned girl came in and peeped into my cage. I recognized her as Elaine, Dr. Takagi's trainee assistant vet.

"Hello Eric, you're up!" she said, stating the obvious, I thought sourly, and, as if she knew what I needed, Elaine filled a small feeding bottle with water and shoved it gently into my mouth. The fresh cold water relieved my dry tongue with its moisture and released it from the roof of my mouth where it had been stuck. I drank greedily and ignored Elaine's pleas to "go slow" and when she tried to pull it away from me, I clamped my teeth tightly down with amazing strength, considering I had just come out of general anesthetic and refused to let go till I had emptied the whole bottle.

"You're going to get me into trouble for sure, Eric. You were supposed to drink slowly, a few sips at a time," Elaine grumbled as she took the empty bottle from me.

I ignored her again because when I want something, I rarely care what people think or say about me. But I did feel a little guilty when I heard Dr. Takagi reprimanding her off for letting me drink so quickly post-surgery and run the risk of choking.

A few minutes later, Dr. Takagi came in to give me a look-over and to test my reflexes. He laughed at my angry response to the pencil he was rotating very impolitely in front of my eyes and pronounced me a little groggy but fully recovered from the general anesthetic with all responses, notably angry ones, intact and absolutely fit to leave the hospital.

Jennifer arrived to take me home an hour later and, in the

excitement of getting my medications sorted out and going over the instructions on how to care for me, she forgot to let me relieve myself before putting me in the car. Oh, boy, my bladder was so full it was fit to burst but wetting the car was something I would never do. It would be too humiliating and disgusting to sink that low, so I doggedly held on.

When we arrived at the parking garage of the condo, I was struggling and grunting from the effort of controlling my bladder. Jennifer realized at last that I urgently needed to relieve myself. She set me gently against a pillar in the parking garage but it wasn't my spot so I refused to do it there.

I have three or four favorite "spots" in the parking garage where I habitually lifted my leg and I wanted a spot that was across the garage. I was so desperate to reach it and ease the agonizing pressure on my bladder that I forgot I had an incapacitated leg; and with amazing dexterity, I scrambled up and hobbled right across the garage on three legs with my bad leg sticking out like a small white stick! Although the circumstances were tragic, I looked so comical that Jennifer burst into giggles and that kind of eased the tension a little.

I didn't even have to lift up my hind leg; it was sticking out in the cast but I couldn't aim properly and got myself all messed up and Jennifer had to clean me. I felt so small and embarrassed that I couldn't even attend to this very personal matter without help from my Mom and resolved to regain my independence as soon as I got used to a life on three legs!

But the ice had been broken so to speak and I was relieved to discover that I could actually move around on three legs quite well. In fact, within a few days, not only could I move around on three legs but I had even mastered the art of doing the song and dance routine on those three legs! And, of course, incurable attention seeker that I am, I loved the crowd of sympathy audience we attracted wherever we went and for that period, I became quite the tragic star of pathos in the condo and enjoyed every minute of it!

Just as she'd done when my front leg was in a cast as a result of my having survived the clamped-down jaws of Cole, the former neighbor's dog, Tanya brought her friends over to admire my cast; they drew all kinds of pictures and even wrote encouraging messages on it!

A week later, my well-decorated hard cast was taken off and the vet put me on a softer cast which was tight and uncomfortable and I wasted no time tearing it off. Jennifer was furious with me because the wound was still raw and we had to rush back to the vet to have another cast put on. I systematically tore off every cast that was put on my leg, piece by piece, and after our third trip to the vet for a replacement cast, all of them, including Dr. Takagi, had had it with me.

They put me in a stiff Elizabethan collar kind of thing so that I could not reach my leg to tear off the soft cast. I was furious and regarded it as dog abuse to trap my head in that hard, plastic lampshade thing. How did they expect any dog to lie down and sleep with that hard lampshade around the neck? And didn't they know that its plastic edge is so sharp that it cuts into the flesh and you feel so claustrophobic inside that hard collar that you can't breathe properly?

I couldn't stand being trapped in that awful collar which weighed me down, restricted my vision and made me teeter on the brink of massive claustrophobia and insanity. No, Jennifer, you can't do this to me, I screamed but she wouldn't listen! So, as usual to get what I wanted, I staged a really big show of hysteria, rolling violently on the floor, banging the collar against the wall and doing anything just to get it off. Only this time, it wasn't all just for show; I was really going into panic attacks.

In the end, Jennifer couldn't stand the sight of me hyperventilating in that collar and was afraid I would hurt myself so she removed it with stern warnings not to tamper with the bandages on my legs. To be fair to me, I tried my best to obey her but I just couldn't hold out for more than thirty minutes.

I absolutely hate to have anything other than my own fur and well, the mandatory collar with my license tag, on my body. Once Jennifer bought a mega-expensive dog T-shirt for me; it was a designer piece her club members were selling and cost a small fortune. Just to make my Mom happy, I let her put it on with every intention of tearing it off the minute her back was turned—which I did, crowning my destructive art with a perfect dissection of the offending T-shirt into ribbons!

When my Mom discovered what I had done, her screams could be heard right across the condo, she was that mad because of the small fortune she had paid for it! But I had made my point; she never attempted to make me wear anything other than my fur and my collar again!

After struggling with my will and my instinct, the latter took over and I crawled into my nest under Tanya's bed to quietly and systematically tear off my bandages. Jennifer always says that I'm at my most dangerous and destructive when I go into hiding and keep very quiet and she is right!

I expected her to be furious but surprisingly she was more resigned than angry, maybe partly because my wound had healed very nicely and was no longer raw and a call to the vet confirmed that it was all right to leave it open. Was I glad that it was over and I could stop fighting with the bandages!

It was fantastic to feel so liberated with my leg freed from the constraints of cast or bandages. Although I stilled hobbled on three legs for the next week or so, putting weight tentatively on my metal-stapled left hind leg only occasionally to try it out, I was obviously on the road to recovery.

At first it felt strange having a leg held together by metal pins and I was afraid to use it in case the pins gave way but as the days passed and I found that there were certain activities or mischief I couldn't get up to with only three legs, I was forced to take the plunge and start using what I privately called my "metal" leg.

Today, my left hind leg is every inch as good as the other three; I am reminded of the pins only when my family jokes about it and says stuff like, when I'm dead, they will find the metal clips in my ashes because metal doesn't burn.

Well, all I can say to that is when I'm dead, I certainly won't care about anything!

CHAPTER | Eighteen

I *am often reminded* that I am "a toy dog," and I absolutely hate that off-handed stereotyping of my breed. It makes me feel like a bimbo.

One day I decided enough was enough and the next person who even breathed the words "toy breed" was going to find out what it felt like to be ravaged by a set of small but piranha-sharp teeth. Who ever came up with that stupid and disrespectful description of a living, breathing being with a heart, a soul and feelings, anyway?

"My, my, this toy dog sure can bite!" cooed one of Jennifer's hapless friends from her reading club playfully that day. But her cooing quickly changed to loud yelps of pain when she realized I meant business.

"I'll show you what a real bite is so we understand each other better next time I allow you to step into this house!" I hissed gleefully as I dug deeper and deeper into that fleshy ankle till I almost touched bone.

I knew I was growing older and looking beyond childish pranks and wicked sarcasm and manipulations for something real and, yes, for something good that I would be remembered for. But with four tiny paws and a body the size and strength of a helpless baby, I wasn't really a candidate for anything significant or substantial and that realization really hit me hard.

Could it be I was slipping into a mid-life crisis and

depression? Jennifer seemed to think so and to my horror I heard serious discussions going on in the family about sending me to a dog therapist!

Wait a minute, didn't only mentally disturbed people see therapists?

"No, I don't need a therapist! See, I'm as sane as anyone else, please don't send me to a shrink!" I shrieked, pawing at Jennifer's lap to get her on my side.

But what do you know, I was misunderstood again as Jennifer ran a hand tenderly through the soft tufts of fur on my head and said, "See, John, even Eric himself agrees he needs help!"

"I don't agree, you nitwit! Why am I always misquoted?" I panted, exasperated, and slunk away to my "I give up" corner behind the computer table to sulk among all the wires of John's latest technology.

"Save me from this humiliation," I prayed and although I have never been the good, law-abiding kind of dog that God loves, for some strange reason, the Almighty decided this time to answer my prayers.

The day started normally enough and at 10 a.m. sharp, Lily, the part-time maid, arrived and as usual, good-naturedly brushed off my "symbolic get rid of the intruder" dance and nip routine.

I am very particular that my family should not get short-changed by anyone so I made sure Lily had started her work and wasn't talking too much on her cell phone before I disappeared to my spot under Tanya's bed for my mid-morning nap.

Hardly twenty minutes later, the sound of the doorbell and the call of duty woke me up. I tried to struggle to my feet because screening the doorbell was my job but the soft blanket I was snuggled in was so comfortable that I considered letting this one go. It was, after all, probably only the postman. Ironically, this was the only time I had ever missed a doorbell when I should not have done that.

Still, old habits or rather old duties die hard. Despite the inviting comfort of the fleece blanket, I could not go back to sleep and waited for the door to slam signaling that the postman had left. But instead, my ears picked up another strange sound. Was that muffled sound Lily crying? Why would she be crying? Something was not right and called for immediate action.

Like a shot, I dashed out to the living room just in time to see the "postman" tying Lily to a chair and when she tried to struggle out of his grip, he brought out a knife and slashed her right across the wrist.

Who was this stranger in the house and how dare he attack Lily on my own turf? Without a thought for my own safety, I hurled myself against the intruder, biting him so hard and deep on his bare ankle that my teeth grated against bone. I am so small that he hadn't seen me and the shock of my sudden attack threw him off balance for a moment but it was enough time for Lily to struggle out of her half-tied ropes. I saw the intruder recovering and going after her and I hurled myself at him again but this time he was ready for me, kicking me so hard that I felt a rib crack and a shot of pain ripped through my body. But I raced right back and caught his leg in another vicious grip, plunging deeper and deeper till my teeth almost broke.

"Run to the front door and go for help, Lily. Run!" I prayed silently. As if she had heard me, Lily somehow managed to get the heavy front door open as she ran out with blood oozing from her cut wrist dripping a red trail.

The intruder tried to go after her but he was hampered by my iron grip on his leg. Although he tried to shake me off, I held on so tightly that he had to practically limp out of the house with me attached just as the security guards whom Lily had alerted on her cell phone gave chase and eventually pinned him down.

"You can let go now, good boy," Shukor, the nice security guard who loved dogs told me. With relief, I released my grip and fell back on the grass in a fiery ball of pain. Lily stumbled over and collapsed right there beside me, her face a pasty white. Someone had called an ambulance and Jennifer because they both arrived at almost the same time. I sank gratefully into the blanket Jennifer had wrapped around me and for once was happy to surrender and let the humans take care of things.

The brutal kicks from the intruder had broken several bones in my body and I lay heavily sedated at the vet's for almost a week, totally unaware that I had become the local hero featured in every newspaper in the city.

"Brave, loyal Pomeranian who, against all odds of his size, fought hard and fearlessly to save the life of the family's maid and helped police capture the robber who has been terrorizing the neighborhood for months with his break-ins."

Some reporters had even taken my picture at the vet's while I lay unconscious and Jennifer showed me the papers when I was allowed to go home. My family was proud of me and I basked in the glow of that pride but most important of all, I had made peace with myself and proved to the whole world that even a "toy dog" could be a hero.

A few weeks later, Tanya pointed out a write-up that pet shops had since reported a big jump in sales of Pomeranians and I was pleased as punch because I had vindicated my species. The additional bonus was that there was no more talk of mid-life crises, depression and dog therapists after that!

CHAPTER | Nineteen

Another year has passed and I am now almost nine years old. The vet says apart from being slightly overweight with a few more gray hairs around my mouth, I am extremely "well preserved." My teeth are intact and white, and I have the agility and behavior of a three-year-old.

"Amazing!" the vet tells Jennifer. "You must be taking extremely good care of him! Pomeranians don't normally have very strong teeth and by this age, they should be in a state of disintegration but just look at those fangs on Eric!"

I look at my Mom triumphantly. "It's the Japanese snacks you grumble so much about. They're filled with minerals and protein and they even polish my teeth as I tear and chew them." I told her so but she ignored me because she's probably embarrassed since she complains so much about how expensive those snacks are and how quickly I go through them.

There's a wicked glint in my eyes as I think about how glad Jennifer must be that I can't make myself understood and tell on her.

But despite my youthful looks and behavior, I think I've matured in the last couple of years. I'm not so impatient and, you know, raring to go all the time. I have more quiet moments and have toned down on all those childish pranks. But it doesn't mean I've gone old and gray. Not at all. At least not in my energy levels. It's just that now I can control my impatience and intolerance when things don't go my way a little better than a few years ago. I'm a little more restrained and I shoot my bullets more selectively now than when I was younger.

My song and dance routines are still as vigorous as ever and my voice not an octave lower; anyone who rings our doorbell still gets a nasty reception. I don't think I can ever stop harassing people who come to our house no matter how much Jennifer pleads with me to stop barking the living daylights out of them because I see it as my job to protect my home and my family. No one seems to understand that but I will soldier on and do what I have to do for as long as I can. The day I stop doing that is the day I'm dead or dying!

So if anyone thinks I am going downhill just because I'm a few years older, they are in for a real surprise! I feel I will never really grow old at least in spirit but there are times when I worry what it will be like for a spirit still yearning for the high jinks to be trapped in an old body in reverse gear and slow motion. But I intend to fight it for as long as I can. Age will take me down eventually but this Pomeranian will go down fighting!

But it's also true that the turning point of my life has arrived and some things are changing. For instance, I am now more cooperative in taking my heart medication because I recognize that it's necessary to keep my heart with its slight murmur well-oiled and in "tick tock" condition so to speak! So I don't play up the way I used to when I was younger, spitting out the tablet or clamping my mouth so tight that Jennifer often threatened to use a pair of pliers to pry it open!

Jennifer is delighted that it's so easy to give me my daily dosage of medication now. She thinks it's because I've mellowed down with age but she doesn't know that I'm far from mellow, or does she think I'm senile? On the contrary, I take my medication and vitamins very willingly now so that I can prolong my youth, vitality, and life for as long as it is medically possible.

"Hey, Mom, I intend to stick around as long I can so bring on the medications and vitamins," I tell her but of course, she doesn't get it. She never gets anything I say! But I will have her know that this Pomeranian still has a whole bag of tricks going for him and the motto "Never say Die even when approached by Death" is what he lives by!

We hadn't met Pop, the ancient Golden Retriever, for several days of walks and I did in passing wonder what had happened to him because in rain, shine or pain, he would insist on his evening walk. I kind of missed him and the feisty spirit that insisted on pushing his aged body forward till it could go no more. He reminded me a little of a very old and much loved vintage car Bill had at the farm and how he used it to the very last no matter how old and slow it got, till one day he started the engine and it spluttered and died down on him after a few hiccoughs, never to move again.

After a week we met Pop's Mom, Yuki, and she told Jennifer very distraughtly that he had finally given up the fight and had slipped into a coma from multi-organ failure brought on naturally by old age. I was disturbed, of course, because Pop was the only dog I could ever reach sniffing distance without going into a frenzy of aggression. Even though he was so old, it was hard to think of him as being lifeless and still. He had always had so much will to move, no matter how laboriously.

After lingering for two days and, unable to stand the anguish of seeing him suffer any more, Pop's family decided to take him to the vet to put him down so that he could go in peace and with dignity instead of a slow labored death in pain and humiliation with urine and excrement flowing indiscriminately out of him.

We were invited to Pop's tearful cremation ceremony after which his ashes were to be put in a pet columbarium attached to the veterinary hospital. Jennifer hesitated taking me along because she knew what kind of havoc I was capable of creating but Pop's parents insisted that I go along. After all, what kind of dog funeral would it be without at least one dog present?

I badly wanted to go and I promised Jennifer I would be good and not mess up anything out of respect for Pop, but she was still doubtful, having suffered the embarrassment of seeing me ruin every occasion I was brought to. I pleaded and bargained and eventually she relented with firm reminders all the way to honor my promises. So I got to attend my first, and only, dog funeral. I was so excited if a little apprehensive.

I hate the vet and hospital atmosphere with its stench of antiseptics, sickness and death and my Mom knows that and of course, she also knows the disruptive danger of making me excited and nervous. So we stayed in the quiet and cool little chapel next to the columbarium and waited for Pop's ashes to arrive, having opted not to watch the actual cremation through a glass window. Even a thrill seeker like me balked at the idea of witnessing such an event!

It was a beautiful little ceremony and since I was the only dog present there was no way I could start a fight or quarrel. Pop's family took turns to read out eulogies to him, lovely, haunting tributes to the dog who had brought so much love, laughter and sunshine into their lives after their two children grew up and left the nest.

With tears in her eyes, Yuki, Pop's Mom, recounted how it was Pop who gave them the love and joy of years of companionship and comfort that they did not receive from their adult children.

I listened to Yuki with mixed feelings, pride and a kind of awe that we dogs can make such a beautiful impact for our human parents to fill the vacuum of disappearing children, and anger that human children can be so selfish and unappreciative of their parents' unconditional love and care. I don't know what is with them. I've heard Jennifer and her friends talk sadly about how all their kids take and take and never give an inch in return. I made a mental note right there at Pop's funeral never to make my Mom cry or feel sad and dejected about me and to be there for her till the end of my days.

And yet Yuki's eulogies were haunting because they made a dog's fifteen years of life on earth seem so inadequate and short, zapping from puppy hood to the precocious young "teen" to the matured responsible adult dog, and finally to the decline and winding down of old age.

I saw Jennifer looking at me and I knew what she was thinking: that somehow I had stopped at the precocious young adult stage, and we both hoped it would stay that way for a long time! We seem to be simultaneously wishing wistfully for the same thing—that my pace of aging would match hers so we could grow old together—but even I, with all my foolhardiness and refusal to face realities, knew that would be impossible.

They made Pop sound like a saint but I didn't buy that! A dog is a dog and surely there must have been times when he chewed up his Dad's favorite shoes or hid the car keys or ransacked his sister's school bag to steal her lunch or made those patches in Mom's precious carpet! Why, every dog has to have done at least one or all of those things to qualify being a dog!

It felt strange that everyone speaks only of the good things of a dog's life after he is dead and all the past sins are instantly forgiven and forgotten. I guess it's probably the same with humans; or is it? Of course, these thoughts circled back to me and I wondered whether people will say good things about me, tongue-in-cheek, when I am dead. I say tongue-in-cheek because everyone knows that my list of "sins," mischief-making and misdemeanors is so long that heck, I myself don't have anything sweet to say about myself! But well, I'm sure my family will come out with something good to say about me because I've heard Jennifer say that one must always say good things about the dead.

Pop's ashes came from the crematorium in a small silver pot and I found it quite incredible that in the end it was all that was left of him, a tiny pile of ashes in a pot! A big dog with size two shoe-sized feet, as Yuki tearfully put it, was now imprisoned in a tiny pot through all eternity! I know someday that will happen to me, too, so I have to live life to the fullest.

I was glad when the funeral was over and we could return to the world of the living. This death thing was much too morbid and depressing for me and I am by nature a very life-orientated dog to whom death is just a remote possibility and the present is more important.

I had had enough reminders of my own immortality for that day and was glad to return to flesh and blood life, away from cremated ashes and eulogies!

CHAPTER | Twenty

One day there was a real buzz in the house and Jennifer became very excited over a pamphlet that had just come in the mail. Excited by the buzz, I climbed up on her knees and tried to snatch the glossy pamphlet away. I couldn't wait to know what was inside especially as it had pictures of dogs on the cover so I knew it involved me in some way!

She ruffled the ridiculous tuft of fur on my head Danny had left behind at the last grooming and laughed, "What a busy body you are, Eric! You want to know everything!"

"Of course, of course!" I panted. "There are lots of dogs on that pamphlet so I should know what you're planning for me!"

She cuffed me again playfully and called John and Tanya over and we pored through the pamphlet together.

"Look," she said. "The range of services for dogs from stress-relieving massages to therapeutic spas complete with Jacuzzis, to day care centers and five star pet hotels with internationally wired web cams! Incredible, isn't it? Dogs have come a long way from when I was a kid and they ate what was left over and slept on old blankets in the kitchen!"

"Indeed! The world has surely gone to the dogs," John quipped.

And suddenly a new craze hit dog owners and lovers everywhere; services to pamper and ease "stressed" dogs! What was even more incredible was how owners got the idea that their dogs were stressed? To be very honest, I think the stress comes from having to put up with all these new-fangled notions that have suddenly hit the pet industry! I should know because Jennifer too got hit by it! And oh, boy, how I first suffered and then lived in the lap of therapy luxury for that!

A group of her friends influenced her into thinking that I was "stressed out" and needed "therapy." I think it was more likely they were stressed out and needed an excuse to amuse themselves partly because their children, including Tanya, were growing up and couldn't be manipulated or incorporated into their way of life anymore. So what better way to amuse themselves but to focus on us, their beloved pet pooches who didn't have voices to protest and fight and would never go away from home? I feel sorry for them, actually, all having to cope with changing lifestyles and learning to live in a vacuum left by "lost" children.

I guess in the end I didn't really kick up a big fuss because I loved my Mom so I just wanted to humor her. If it made her happy to "dog spa" me, so be it! Besides, she always decides what is good for me and like most dogs, I have very little say in the scheme of things so it's much easier in the end to go along with her. And okay, I hate to admit it but I was more than a little curious about this craze that was razing the pet community like a raging bush fire. It tickled me pink to see those glossy brochures of dogs lying in tubs of bubbling water surrounded by flowers and glowing tea candles. What were all those humans thinking of?

After mulling over it for a while, Jennifer finally overcame an initial hesitation at such excesses in pet care and booked an appointment for me at one of the dog spas which touted itself as a "dog retreat and sanctuary." It had been difficult to decide which one to choose from all the claims of "services fit for a royal dog," "testimonies of satisfied pooches" and "your dog is our command!" Even the advertisements were amusing and downright bizarre!

My Mom knew she was taking a risk here because there was no telling what I could do to turn even a dog sanctuary into a war zone. But she was banking on the fact that I was a lot older since my last social gathering and matured enough to handle an event designed to calm and soothe dog senses and not set them on fire. John and Tanya were more skeptical and cautious about my "maturity" to handle such a high-risk activity and listed all the possible casualties, the bites I could inflict on the masseuses, the number of things I could break and damage at the spa but Jennifer had become as curious as I was and decided to go ahead.

Anyway, I was going through a "good boy" patch after the sobering experience of Pop's funeral so I resolved to give Jennifer a pleasant surprise by conforming for the first time, at least while this patch lasted. My "good boy" stints don't usually last very long after which I usually go into an overdrive of "bad boy" high jinks and just drive Jennifer totally up the wall!

"When will you ever grow up?" she groans at me, forgetting that I am not only grown up but steadily entering the hallway of dog middle age! As she often consoles herself, maybe that's one of my charms, that I never seem to grow up and thus stay forever her little boy!

The spa was a luxurious place right from the entrance, all tinted glass and cool shady plants, "a Zen kind of atmosphere," as the receptionist at the beautiful kidney-shaped reception counter explained loftily to us. I stifled a giggle because she made it sound as if all their dog patrons can actually tell the difference between "Zen" and "non-Zen," so to speak.

I could see my Mom being quite overwhelmed by the splendid trappings of a, what was it, dog retreat and sanctuary?

Even I was a little dumbstruck by the opulence of an establishment for animals, usually considered the world's second or third class citizens but I wasn't going to show myself up to the smug, aloof receptionist.

"Gosh, what a schmuck!" I thought, and pawed Jennifer on the arm.

"Hey, Mom, don't look so, you know, hillbilly. We have to act as if coming to a five star dog spa is something we do all the time!"

I stared back at the snooty receptionist with that haughty tilt of my head I always put on when I want to appear aloof, every inch the champion bloodline specimen my papers say I am. Good Lord, what had she to be so snooty about? We were the patrons and the paying clients, after all! That at least subdued her and I fancied she looked at us with new respect. I slanted a look at my Mom and closed my left eye slowly in a surreptitious wink. I had put Miss Snooty Pants in her place and I was pleased as punch about that.

I could tell Jennifer was amused by the way the corners of her mouth lifted ever so slightly but she gave a small affected shudder and reminded me with her eyes of my promises to behave like a gentleman, just in case my little victory got into my head.

Jennifer filled in a card with all my personal details, allergies and even my likes and dislikes, and then we were taken inside for another shock. Polished stone walkways with little artificial waterfalls and Japanese stone lanterns and clumps of leafy indoor plants greeted us and we felt as if we had died, left our cluttered world and gone to a paradise of space, tranquility and what must surely be the "Zen" atmosphere the lofty receptionist had spoken about. It was a heavenly place!

For once even what Jennifer calls my ever-ready voice chords were silenced and I was too overwhelmed to make my usual snide provocative comments when a beribboned poodle sashayed past with selected tufts of fur on her tail and face dyed a rosy pink! I stole a look at Jennifer whose jaws were literally dropping!

Another Tshih Tzu glided past, hair drawn back from her face and styled in elaborate curls that were held together by a clip literally dripping with colored stones and diamantes which looked too heavy for the poor mutt's head! I refer to all these dogs as female simply because I can't imagine any self-respecting male dog allowing himself to be made over like that! Were these humans nuts or what? This time my own jaws were dropping, too, and much to Jennifer's relief that kept me quiet! But we had already paid for our "full services dog" package at the spa and we intended to make complete use of it.

If I could keep a diary or have access to an online blog, I would have entered this as "Eric's Unforgettable Day at the Spa."

My most spectacular metamorphosis was the feeling of calm that the ambience of the place flooded into my normally overheated system, discreetly removing all traces of aggression and hostility. For the first time in my life, I was able to be around other dogs without making a single move to challenge or provoke!

Somehow, even I, Eric the Terror, could not bring myself to create a noise and destroy the ambience and serenity of the place and its relaxing and de-stressing guests!

Jennifer, too, was surprised because I have never been known to let any dog go by without some show of aggression and in fact she had already made provision for that by booking a single room for us.

We started with the massage therapy, an exercise made in heaven itself! A young lady smelling of flowers and aromatherapy oils slithered silently into the room, placed me on a soft, fleecy white towel, and started to work her magic fingers on my body from head to back to tail.

Oh, to feel the tight muscles unwinding and those little pricks of pain I have these days when I run too much just melting away! I take back every nasty word I have ever said about male dogs that enjoy such frivolous activities being fags! And I take my hat off to the people who invented spas for dogs!

Normally, I make a big noisy fuss about taking my shower and our weekly session always ends up in a wet wrestling match between Jennifer and me in the bathtub. Nothing, neither threats nor bribes can make me submit peacefully to my ten-minute shower quickies and I always give hell to my Mom. As soon as I can struggle out of the bath tub, I jump onto her bed where I shake all the remaining water from my body and after this, I proceed to rub my wet body all over her bed sheets and pillows to thoroughly dry myself. This is my way of punishing Jennifer for making me take a bath against my will. It really infuriates her but there is nothing she can do because I'm always much faster than her!

But here, in this canine paradise, the bubbling water with its sweet smelling flower petals floating around just makes a dog want to jump in and that was what I did. This was my first Jacuzzi with its therapeutic bubbling water gently massaging and kneading my body, and I loved every minute of being immersed in that warm, scented water! Of course, I couldn't resist tearing the flowers floating around me into shreds and later putting out a paw to trip a real snooty Tshih Tzu who acted as if she were the Empress Dowager, but those were about the only casualties of my day at the dog spa, which was very good, considering my usual record.

I came home that evening a new dog and I showed my appreciation to Jennifer for the experience by suppressing all my basic instincts and being almost an exemplary dog for exactly three days. Although my Mom's official stand was that she wished she could afford to send me to the spa every three days so that I would always behave, I knew deep inside she was glad to have her "Eric the Terror" back. As Tanya said, despite causing so much "wear and tear" I was definitely more entertaining being a bad boy than a good one.

Jennifer knew I had really enjoyed myself that day and promised to give me a treat at the dog spa on special occasions like my birthday because only rich widows and heiresses like Paris Hilton could afford to send their dogs more frequently. But do you know what? I wouldn't trade Jennifer and the rest of my family for all the rich widows, heiresses and dog spas in the world!

Another thing I love is the Christmas season. It's all the hustle and bustle of the Christmas shopping and the presents and watching my Mom go through endless brochures of Christmas turkey for our Christmas Eve dinner. And even though I can't go on Christmas shopping sprees with Jennifer because those misguided shopping complexes don't allow dogs in, it's still exciting to see her and the rest of the family coming back with bags and bags of good old "Christmas cheer."

Of course I always want to be a part of the present wrapping rituals although I can't do much except to create more Christmas "spirit" by snatching cellophane tapes, scissors and bits of discarded Christmas wrappers! And of course, they have a present for me, too, and although I apply my best hunting "intelligence" skills all over the house, I never find it till Christmas Eve. This year, I will search the car, too, because I'm convinced by now that if it's not anywhere and I mean anywhere in the house, Jennifer must be hiding it in the car!

It's great fun to listen to her swear every year that *this* year things were going to be different, that instead of the usual turkey and common Christmas fare, she would organize something extraordinary. And you know what? To my great relief, because I simply love turkey, it never happens! After a couple of weeks pounding all the Christmas food shops and piles of glossy brochures, Jennifer inevitably comes back on the afternoon of Christmas Eve lugging a giant seven-kilo turkey!

I have absolutely no idea why my Mom makes such promises of "extraordinary" dinners in vain but it happens every year, without fail, like clockwork on oiled wheels!

Why a family of just three people plus a fifteen pound dog would need fifteen pounds of turkey is explained airily away as Christmas is the season for excesses and even if half of that giant turkey stays in the freezer for the rest of the year, Jennifer wouldn't hear of anything smaller!

It's fantastic when they start putting up the Christmas tree and the mess I create for everyone, stealing and hiding the bright decorative baubles and the sparkling white snow angels and running off with the gold and silver banners for the door when Jennifer's back is turned.

But there is one rule that even I dare not break. It's still acceptable that I fool around as much as I want as long as I can take Jennifer's nagging while they are putting up the tree but the minute the tree is up and all the decorations are in place, I can touch anything only on pain of death. And this may have a ring of truth to it because they normally light up the tree with multi-colored electric Christmas lights and Jennifer always warns me that I can be electrocuted if I go near the tree.

I never found out whether that was really true or only a scare tactic to keep the tree safe from me but I wasn't going to take any chances! Being electrocuted to a charred mass was not my idea of Christmas "cheer" for dogs!

Except one Christmas, when Jennifer received a whole box of the gaily striped Christmas candy in the shape of canes and since no one wanted to eat the sweets in anticipation of better Christmas fare, Tanya suggested hanging them on the tree and because she didn't want the heat of the electric lights to melt the candy sticks, that year, Jennifer didn't put lights on the tree.

I love sweets and I guess you already know how this is going to go! With a whole bunch of sweets hanging tantalizingly on a tree doing nothing, some of which I could easily reach and without the threat of electrocution to scare me off, the temptation was just too great and I was able to hold back for just one day.

The next day, the sweet smell of the many candy sticks hanging on the tree became irresistible and before I knew it, I had reached up and pulled down a couple of sticks. The pressure of my tugging brought the light artificial tree that Jennifer had opted for that year together with all the decorations down and I watched with horror as Christmas tinsel, baubles and candy sticks rolled and scattered in all directions!

When Jennifer came back, there was hell to pay and although she didn't lay a finger on me, she has this special way of ranting at me till I feel very small and finally shrink to a pint-size Pomeranian mass with a brain the size of a peanut indeed!

I sat patiently through a whole thirty minutes of the special Christmas edition of her brain-scorching diatribe before she put me on a chair and made me sit there in a sentry-like pose to watch her putting the tree back together again, without making a single sound or movement.

I never dared go near the tree that whole Christmas because I couldn't trust myself not to pull it down again. By way of punishment, Jennifer had hung back all the candy sticks just to teach me a lesson in restraint!

Needless to say, that wasn't my best Christmas but I know my Mom felt bad about being so mean to me because that year, I got the best Christmas presents—toys to play with and to tear to pieces, snacks, and everything a dog could wish for!

I also got a double helping of turkey and what I suspected was a larger than usual slab of fabulous Christmas log cake with, lo and behold, a gaily striped candy stick gracing my plate! Jennifer even gave me a couple of sips of champagne which made me feel wonderfully giggly and light-headed!

I forgave her, of course, and Christmas that year ended with its usual good cheer and spirit after all!

And as part of our round the table Christmas Eve champagne-influenced dinner conversation, Jennifer commented on the incongruity of a dog who does something wrong like pulling down a whole Christmas tree and being punished quite rightly for it and then somehow manages to make his Mom feel bad and the guilty one for meting out that punishment to him!

I stumbled into bed that night, a drunk dog because I had managed to persuade my "guilt ridden" Mom to extend her offer of champagne to more than the few sips she had intended.

And as usual, in our family, the dog always wins the day!

CHAPTER | Twenty-One

Recently I came across some pictures of the first Eric in the family and I started thinking a great deal about this guy for whom I was selected and named, to keep his memory alive.

Jennifer keeps his pictures in two albums in a side cupboard and one boring afternoon, I was able to drag one of the albums out and turn the pages with my teeth. Magnificent job! I felt extremely proud of myself!

My Mom never gets tired of telling the story of Eric 1. The family had never kept a dog so when a close friend pleaded with them to adopt a neglected Pomeranian, they were reluctant because having to care for a pet would hinder their love for impromptu traveling. But the Pomeranian badly needed even a temporary shelter so could Jennifer just take him in for just a few days while they tried to find him another home, pleaded the friend. He himself couldn't take in the Pomeranian because his pair of Spitz would never allow that.

She finally relented and Eric 1 arrived that evening in nothing fancier than an old, brown cardboard box. He was very tiny for a grown dog, merely the size of a book, and when the family peered excitedly into the box; he was so frightened he started to shiver violently. Jennifer's heart went out to the timid little dog who seemed frightened of everything, even her voice.

All kinds of loud noises especially the cracking sounds of thunder and lightning freaked him out and he would just run to

Jennifer and cower in her arms at the slightest hint of any kind of force. They reckoned he must have been battered and beaten up badly by his previous owners at least a few times to be so terrified of force or loud noises of any sort.

My family never stops telling me how different I am from my predecessor. I am not at all afraid of thunder and loud noises, far from that, I am a thrill seeker and loud cracking sounds excite me! Once a year, there is a celebration in the streets of our neighborhood and fireworks and crackers are fired right through the night till daybreak and my family was surprised that instead of cowering from the sharp cracking sounds and the flying sparks, I am thrilled and intrigued by them and would pester Jennifer or anyone in the family to take me to the streets and central square to watch the fascinating display of fireworks. The louder the crackers and the higher the sparks flew, the more excited I got!

Jennifer can only shake her head and wonder how a small dog can be such a thrill seeker when the other much bigger and stronger dogs are whining and hiding in their homes!

In fact, the only thing I had in common with Eric 1 was our Pomeranian breed.

Anyway, Eric 1 was a lovely dog, eager to please and so obedient it seemed he lived to serve. He had never received so much love and care especially the kind Jennifer lavished on him and till the day he died, he loved her so much that he lived only for her. When she was away, he pined for her and when she was around, his eyes followed her everywhere.

At the end of a week, the friend told Jennifer he had found a home for Eric but by then she and the whole family had become so attached to him, they couldn't bear to give him up. They made all kinds of excuses to keep him: he needed a lot of love and care, both medical and emotional, and they worried that his new owner might not have the patience to give him that. Besides, he was just beginning to gain a little confidence in himself and it would set him back a lot and send him creeping back to his shell again if they changed his environment at this point.

So Eric 1 came to the family for a week of temporary shelter and stayed for ten years till he died. But his former life of neglect had already taken its toll on him and his heart, teeth and internal organs were ticking time bombs. For the rest of his life, Eric 1 had to take five different kinds of medication and even then, he had periodic heart and respiratory attacks that sent Jennifer and John rushing to the animal hospital, sometimes at all hours of the night.

Even before I raided the albums, my Mom had shown me photos of Eric 1. Of course, he had the same Pomeranian markings as me but there, the resemblance ended. I am as strong as an ox with what Jennifer calls a hawkish face and the perfect build and coat that come with the best nutrition that money can buy, whereas, Eric 1 had a very sweet but wan looking face, and a disastrous body. His poor diet had left him with weak hind legs and very bad teeth and no amount of grooming and vitamins could improve his coat. His tail didn't curl up gloriously in a typically Pomeranian plume like mine, but had disintegrated into a twig covered by a smattering of dry, scraggy fur. Jennifer said it was due to poor circulation and the tail was drying up because not enough blood reached it.

We were also poles apart in character and personality. Eric 1 was timid and diffident and he didn't have a lot of confidence in himself. And although he trusted Jennifer and the rest of the family completely and without reservations, the deep scars inflicted by his previous owners could never really be wiped out and he crumbled easily.

In fact, Tanya told me that all you had to say was "Boo" and he would start trembling.

I was intrigued by the story of my namesake and how Jennifer suffered the roller coaster of good days and very bad health days in the last year of his life till one day, she couldn't take it anymore, the sight of him in constant pain made her realize how selfish she was to keep him alive in any condition for her own sake although every vet she saw told her he was suffering terribly and she had to put him down to release him from a world of pain that not even drugs could relieve and it was going to get worse as the days went by.

I have no patience for pain and suffering but Eric 1 was different. He had a great capacity to endure suffering and could remain quite stoic even in extreme pain which would have seen me screaming the roof down.

I realized that he had a very strong will which sort of overcame his very bad physical condition when Jennifer told me the story of how Eric 1 flew to Japan when they were assigned there for five years and at the end of that period, even with a very bad heart and near-handicapped hind legs and back, he endured the six-hour plane journey back plus the one month in quarantine confinement to stay with his beloved family for another two years. No one expected him to survive the plane journey back or the one-month quarantine, not even the quarantine officers, who advised Jennifer to put him down the minute he arrived from Japan.

But that iron will to live for his family beat all the odds and Eric 1 not only came out of quarantine as well as could be expected in the circumstances but also lived for two more years!

But on February 25th, 1998, he had come to the end of the road and could no longer go on and even Jennifer realized that and gave up the battle. On the day she was to take him to the vet, Jennifer bathed Eric 1 tenderly, gave him his favorite fruit of papaya, as much as he wanted and brought him to the toilet to relieve himself. Unlike me, she had to carry him around for real because by then he could no longer walk.

Jennifer handed him to the vet, tears streaming down her face; I mean, it was a horrible thing for her, to be there, asking the vet to take away the life of the creature she loved so much. But the last look he gave her was one of assurance and absolute trust that she was doing the right thing for him. It was a heart wrenching and haunting moment that would never be forgotten.

"See you in fifty years," Jennifer whispered and not trusting herself to witness the "procedure" and the cremation after that, she bolted from the clinic, leaving John to settle the details and expenses.

The family swore never to have a pet again because the pain of seeing it grow old and die was just too great but within days of Eric 1's passing, the great hollow left by him and the barren atmosphere of a pet-less house was too much and by the weekend, everyone admitted defeat and went prowling the pet shops for an Eric look-alike replacement. And that was how they found me.

I felt so spoiled and vain after hearing the story of Eric 1 and resolved to be a better dog but like. all my past resolutions, it didn't last beyond forty-eight hours!

Jennifer admitted that she had expected me to be sweet-natured and patient like Eric 1 and had been quite shocked at how I turned out: loud-mouthed, aggressive, bad-tempered, and a law unto myself, listening to no one and doing exactly as I pleased. Probably if she could understand dog language, she would be horrified at how foul mouthed I can be, too; how else does she think I provoke the other dogs until they want to tear my guts out?

That is how Pomeranians really are, she was told. Eric 1 had been unusually mild-tempered and not typical of the breed, possibly because his spirit had been completely broken by his previous life of abuse and neglect. But eventually I convinced them how much more interesting a feisty dog like me could be and I don't think they would have me any other way. I know, because sometimes when I'm a bit under the weather and become unusually quiet and lethargic, they get worried. My Mom always believes if I am not my usual feisty self, there has to be something wrong with me! And she is right, of course; if I feel like my usual self, no one can catch me quiet and doing much soul searching and reflecting on my life!

But sometimes when Jennifer gets real frustrated with my defiance and having to soothe a lot of ruffled feathers and fur outside, she would burst out, "Why can't you be more like old Eric? Such a gentleman he was!"

"He was what he was, angel, saint reincarnated and I am what I am, none of us can help being what we are and I'm glad to be Eric, Rogue Pomeranian so let's live and let live!" I retorted, but I don't think she understood me.

Well, they don't say it's a dog's life of being misunderstood, misinterpreted and misquoted for nothing!

CHAPTER | Twenty-Two

Something unbelievable is happening to me. I think I've grown old, very old. I hear my Mom going out and I want to run to the door, do my song and dance number as I used to do, but my legs won't move.

After a while, I try again and this time, I can get up but I must do it slowly because my legs seem to have gone very stiff, like stick, and I have this great weight on me that makes my whole body feel leaden. It's not the fur this time but a kind of heavy feeling, as if someone has slit open my body and filled it with stones. By the time I get to the door, Jennifer has left and after a while I have to lie down again to rest; even walking to the door is too much for me.

Where did the years go and when did I grow so old? I hate being elderly and slow. My body can't keep up with my mind and all the things I still want to do. My eyesight is failing and I think Jennifer mentioned that my eyes are turning white with cataract. I wouldn't know because I refuse to look at the mirror any more. I can't bear to see myself even if I could make it to the mirror in Jennifer's room.

My eyes become misty with longing as I remember the times a few short years ago that I used to march up to preen and pirouette in front of that same gilt framed ornate mirror, a shameless narcissist proud of my perfectly poised body and Pomeranian markings. I was an orange and gold glory to behold!

And now it's all gone. I can't believe I'm this crippled, dull beige, graying and decrepit dog mass!

I know Jennifer is trying desperately to prolong my life because my family can't bear to lose me: vitamins, visits to the vet the minute I cough or have one of my breathless attacks. But it won't really do any good. I can feel the energy and essence of life slowly seeping away from my body and, day by day, I'm growing weaker and losing even the will to fight.

There is a twist to the saying "every dog has his day" and I know my day comes nearer with every sunset and sunrise. I don't want to die or to grow old; I want to be young and vibrant forever but I know it's impossible. Every night I go to sleep afraid that I won't be able to get up the next day and sometimes the rheumatic pains get so bad I think it's better to end it all. But Jennifer refuses to give up. She rubs all kinds of ointments on my legs to ease the pain and that helps for a while.

I still love to go out, drinking in the sights and sounds of the world outside, and Jennifer carries me to the gardens downstairs at least two or three times a day. Now she has to carry me for real. I regret the times in the past that I played all those tricks to make her carry me simply because I was too lazy to walk and the view from her height was much better than the view from one foot above the ground!

Oh, I would give anything now to be able to spring out of her arms and walk or run on my own. I never realized that I would have time enough to be carried around when I became aged and gray. I remember what Pop, the old Golden Retriever who died quite a few years ago, told me once that I should walk while I still could because there would be plenty of time to be carried around later. And he's right, of course. I have realized that too late!

My eyes pick out the shrubs Tanya and I used to play hide

and seek behind, racing around at breakneck speed, and the wooden benches under the swaying palm trees where we used to sit down, panting, to rest. It is amazing and unfair how the gardens, even the benches, stay frozen in time, unchanged. But how we, the higher forms of life have to change, grow old, sick and weak!

Look at me: I am gray and weak and my voice comes out in frail plaintive barks where it used to shriek like a banshee or roar like a tiger depending on what the occasion called for! And Tanya is grown up and gone from the family, starting her own life with the nonchalance and willfulness of the young. I guess she hardly thinks of me or Jennifer anymore!

I know that my Mom feels as I do, that time has passed us too swiftly. Why, oh why, can't we go back to the time when Tanya was young and innocent and the simple joys of life were enough for her and she thought the world of her Mom? Now they fight all the time and Jennifer turns to me with a fierce intensity that will be much harder for her to let go when the time comes for me to leave this world. How can I leave her when she has done so much for me? But I am defeated by the very time I swore to fight against when I was young and fearless!

We still have many moments of joy, cuddling together on the couch when we watch TV together, or in bed before she gently puts me on the nest of blankets she still makes for me at her feet so that she will not accidentally hurt me when she turns and tosses at night. We laugh a lot when we go to the park and watch the other dogs fooling around, remembering the time when I was Eric the Terror, and she enjoys watching me when we go for car rides and I still manage to stand up on my hind legs to watch the world go by.

"Watch out for dogs!" Jennifer would say when she sees other dogs going for their walks, and I will still do what I did before, leaping at the car window to "get" at the dogs who "dare to walk my earth." Although the leaps are now slow and feeble and the barks thin, my spirit is still there, as strong as ever, and that's good enough for Jennifer.

"Good catch today right, Eric?" she coos and I look at her, the triumphant "I win" grin which used to irritate so many people and dogs, back on my face.

I want such moments to last forever. I've really grown sentimental and daft in my old age, and there was a time when I would never have the patience for such sentiments! Well, those times are gone and here I am, a decrepit shadow of my former self! I remember Pop, the old retriever, grunting to me that "when you're young, you have a whole life and future to wake up to each day for; but when you get old, there's only memories to look back on each day." At that time, I hardly bothered about anything he said because nothing could dampen my high spirits but now it's all coming back to roost, and there's not a thing I can do to stop the clock ticking.

I can't even eat the snacks on my own anymore; Jennifer has to break them up into tiny pieces for me. Tell me, how much more humiliating can old age be? Sometimes I can't even control my bowels and make messes literally "in my pants." Jennifer never scolds me for such accidents but I can see she is sad because the younger Eric was so particular about personal hygiene he would never dream of making messes like that. It just showed how much I was losing control of myself.

In fact, I used to empty my bowels once a day like clockwork, around mid-morning, and each time I did it, I would wipe my backside on a piece of newspaper till I was sure it was absolutely clean. My family used to joke about me being a self-cleansing dog and when you consider that I wash my own eyes, face and ears each day, they had a point there! How I used to scoff at those dogs downstairs who had to be wiped down by their owners every day!

I know how it will end. One day I will wake up and find that I have become too weak to get up. I will lie there in a pool of urine and whine for help. Jennifer will come running and she will gently carry me to the bathroom sink to clean me up, stroking me all the time and telling me it's okay even though we both know it's not and never will be okay.

This has happened for one week running and today I can't even eat. All the old aches and pains seem to converge in my body, squeezing the life out of it. I know it's time to let go and head for the inevitable, the final visit to the vet. I can't stand the indignity of going on with life like this any more, no matter how much I hate to leave this world and my beloved parents, and I understand at last why it's kinder to put down a dog in my condition. And yet, I'm so afraid to die, to let go and drift into the unknown. It's coming, the final visit to the vet, my body is dead but my mind is still alive, trapped in this carcass that refuses to set me free.

"I must get out of this prison! Help me, someone, help me!" I scream over and over again. There is a scuffle of noises around me and I scream louder for help.

Someone is shaking me and I open my eyes to see Jennifer peering at me and saying, "Did you see Eric screaming and thrashing? He must be having a nightmare!"

Yes, I am thrashing and I can move and stand up fast and I'm as agile as I have always been!

"I'm not old!" my heart sings. "The horrors of old age and that trip to the vet that every dog dreads, it was all a dream!"

"I'm still alive, young and intact!" I scream as I proceed to try my song and dance routine, not caring about the way Jennifer looks at me. Probably she thought I had gone mad, getting into my song and dance number for no apparent reason which I had never done before. She couldn't possibly understand how I had gone through the trauma of old age and the final trip to the vet before being brought back from that abyss of death to find myself young and bursting with vitality again.

I check my legs and my face in the mirror. Everything is perfect and in good working condition! Jennifer hadn't taken me for a session with Danny yet and my fur had grown out to a magnificent halo of gold with my prominent Pomeranian tail curved back over my back in a glorious arc. I can't believe how good I look! I want it to last forever!

Now I wish Jennifer wouldn't take me to Danny's so fast to shear off all my golden locks. I know it's hot to carry all that fur on me but I look so good, I am prepared to suffer the heat! I want to look this good for as long as I can!

Jennifer doesn't know why I have become kinder, less impertinent and more humble. Sometimes she teases me about it: I was really growing more mellow with old age.

"Stop talking about old age, woman!" I growl at her.

"That's the spirit, boy! That's my Eric!" she laughs and I realize how much she misses the gung-ho, feisty and devil-may-care old me! And I'm determined to cast aside this shadow of old age that has been trailing me since that terrifying dream and live the life of Eric, The Terror for as long as I can...ironically, I know my Mom expects that of me!

I laugh back, shaking my head at my Mom. These humans! Which dog can understand them? Ever since I could remember my family, including Jennifer, has always moaned and groaned about my rebellious and irreverent behavior but now that I have decided to be more of the "model dog" they had always wished for, they want my old crackpot cantankerous self back, dents, warts and all! And, boy, was I glad to oblige them and be myself again, my real self!

So I decided to throw off the "good boy" mantle I was beginning to tire of anyway and return to what I did best, terrorizing all around me with my cranky and arm wrestling tactics complemented by the high-octave vocal chords that the years had not been able to tame.

Let the future and old age and death take care of itself. Why do I think so much about something I cannot control? For now, I still have a lot of living to do!

ABOUT The Author

Rei Kimura, born and raised in Tokyo, is a lawyer-turned-writer currently associated with the Australian News Syndicate. Author of several published novels, including *Butterfly in the Wind, Japanese Magnolia*, and *Awa Maru, Titanic of Japan*, Kimura now lives and works in Singapore. Her novels have been published in many languages including Dutch, Spanish, Hungarian, Russian, Polish, Hindi, Marathi, Thai, Indonesian, Korean, Japanese, Vietnamese, and Chinese.